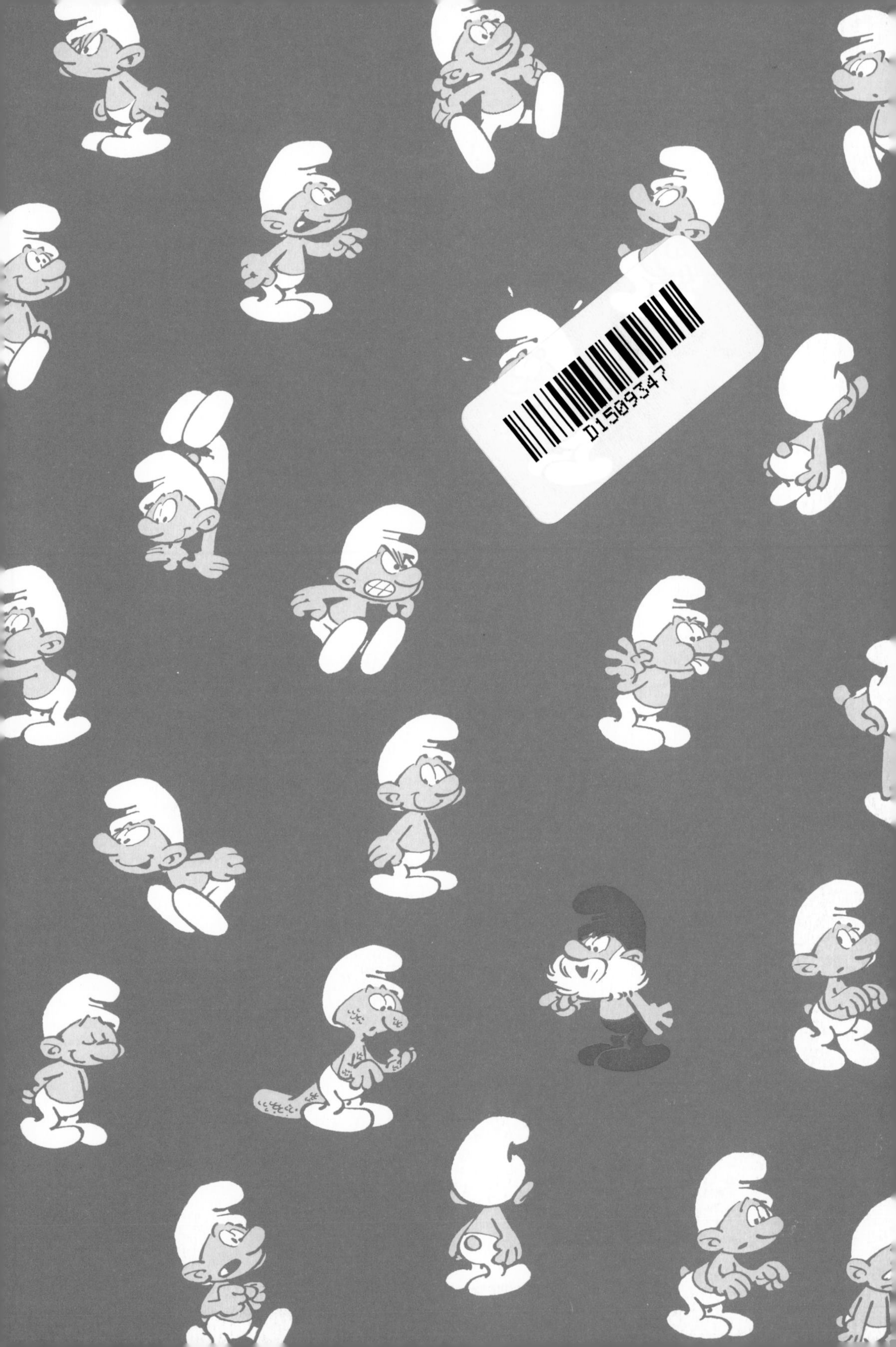

THE SMURF APPRENTICE

Peyo

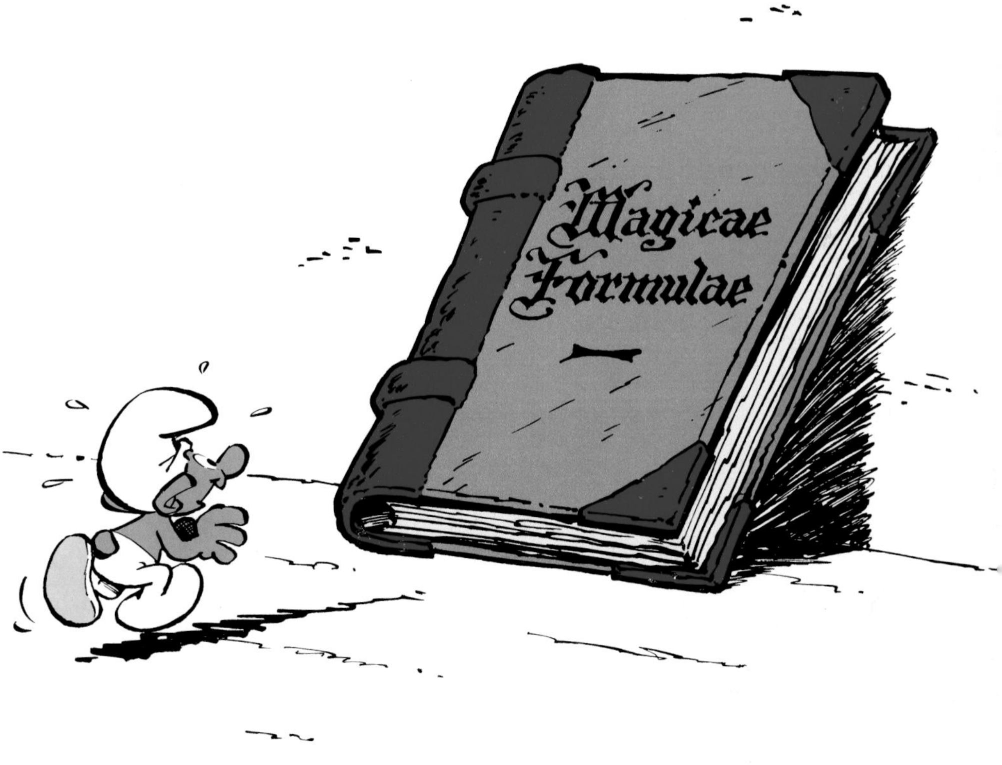
Magicae Formulae

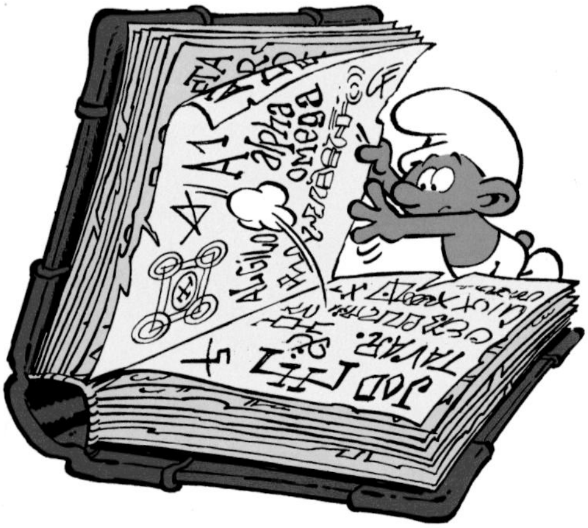
alpha
omega

THE SMURF APPRENTICE

I heat it...
And presto! It's ready!
I pour it on this seed and...
BOOM

A SMURFS GRAPHIC NOVEL BY Peyo

PAPERCUTZ™
NEW YORK

 **SMURFS** GRAPHIC NOVELS AVAILABLE FROM **PAPERCUTZ** ™

1. THE PURPLE SMURFS
2. THE SMURFS AND THE MAGIC FLUTE
3. THE SMURF KING
4. THE SMURFETTE
5. THE SMURFS AND THE EGG
6. THE SMURFS AND THE HOWLIBIRD
7. THE ASTROSMURF
8. THE SMURF APPRENTICE

COMING SOON:

9. GARGAMEL AND THE SMURFS
10. THE RETURN OF THE SMURFETTE
11. THE SMURF OLYMPICS

The Smurfs graphic novels are available in paperback for $5.99 each and in hardcover for $10.99 each at booksellers everywhere.

Or order through us. Please add $4.00 for postage and handling for the first book, add $1.00 for each additional book. Please make check payable to NBM Publishing. Send to: PAPERCUTZ, 40 Exchange Place, Suite 1308, New York, NY 10005 (1-800-886-1223).

WWW.PAPERCUTZ.COM

THE SMURF APPRENTICE

SMURF™ © Peyo - 2011 - Licensed through Lafig Belgium -
English translation Copyright © 2011 by Papercutz.
All rights reserved.

"The Apprentice Smurf"
BY PEYO

"Smurf Traps"
BY PEYO AND GOS

"The Smurfs and the Mole"
BY PEYO

Joe Johnson, SMURFLATIONS
Adam Grano, SMURFIC DESIGN
Janice Chiang, LETTERING SMURFETTE
Matt. Murray, SMURF CONSULTANT
Michael Petranek, ASSOCIATE SMURF
Jim Salicrup, SMURF-IN-CHIEF

PAPERBACK EDITION ISBN: 978-1-59707-279-3
HARDCOVER EDITION ISBN: 978-1-59707-280-9

PRINTED IN CHINA SEPTEMBER 2011 BY WKT CO. LTD.
3/F PHASE I LEADER INDUSTRIAL CENTRE
188 TEXACO ROAD, TSEUN WAN, N.T., HONG KONG

DISTRIBUTED BY MACMILLAN
FIRST PAPERCUTZ PRINTING

THE APPRENTICE SMURF

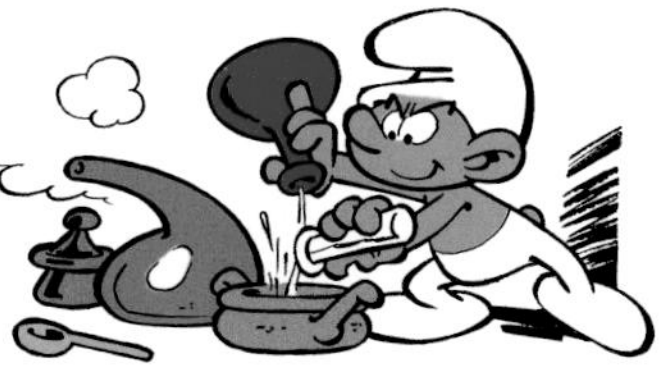

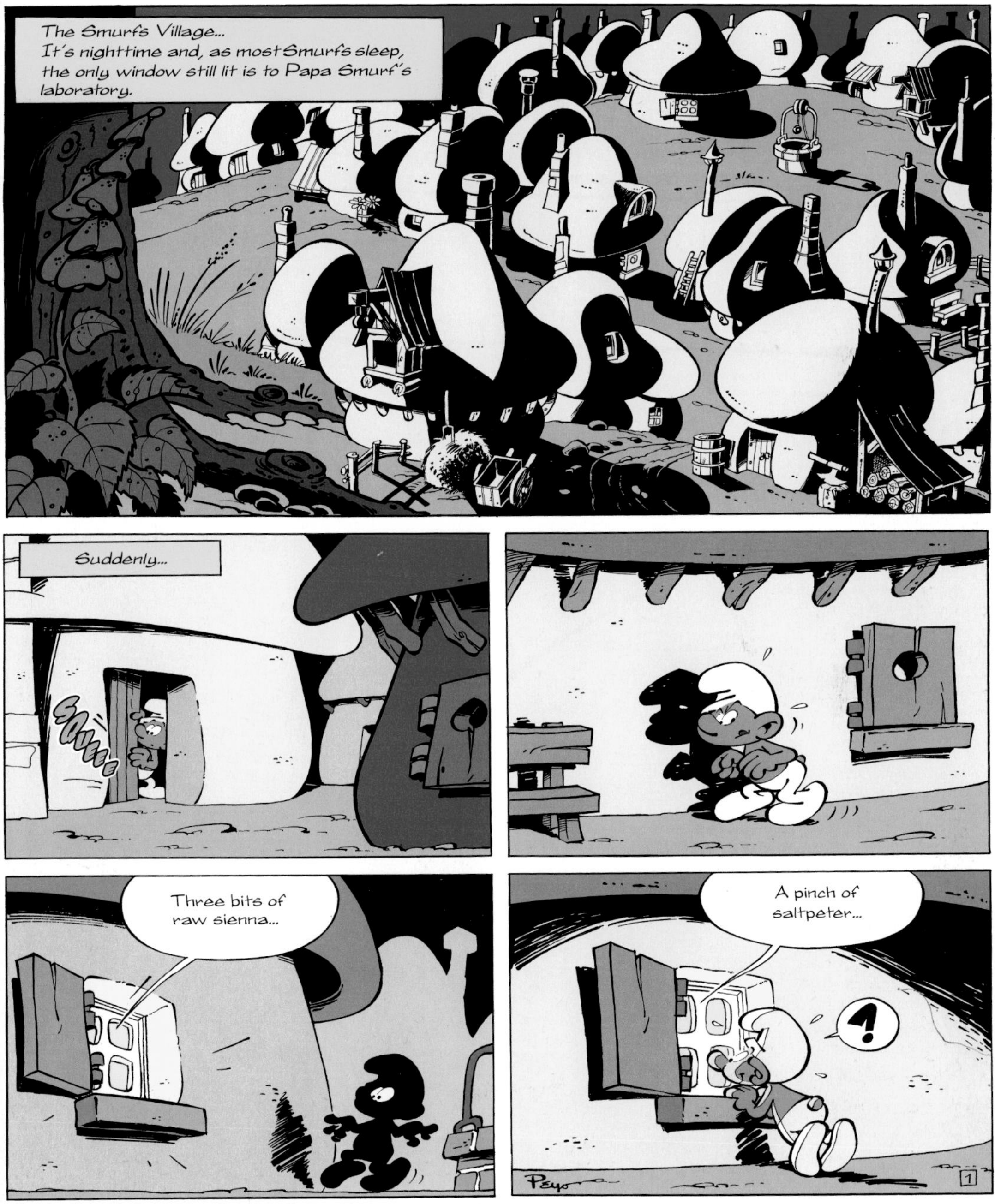
The Smurfs Village...
It's nighttime and, as most Smurfs sleep, the only window still lit is to Papa Smurf's laboratory.
Suddenly...
SQUEEE
Three bits of raw sienna...
A pinch of saltpeter...
?
1

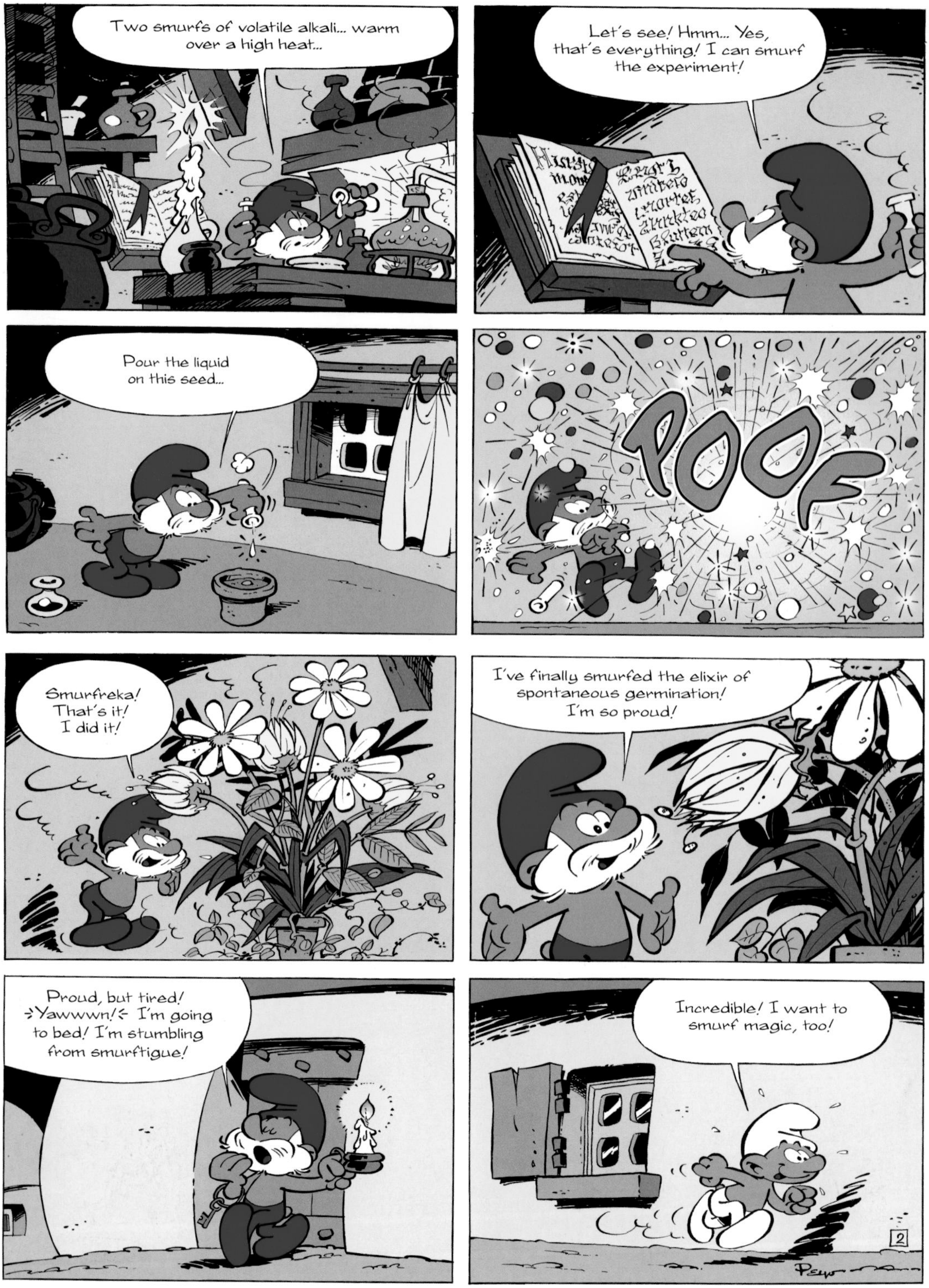
Two smurfs of volatile alkali... warm over a high heat...
Let's see! Hmm... Yes, that's everything! I can smurf the experiment!
Pour the liquid on this seed...
POOF
Smurfreka! That's it! I did it!
I've finally smurfed the elixir of spontaneous germination! I'm so proud!
Proud, but tired! ⩾Yawwwn!⩽ I'm going to bed! I'm stumbling from smurftigue!
Incredible! I want to smurf magic, too!
2
Peyo

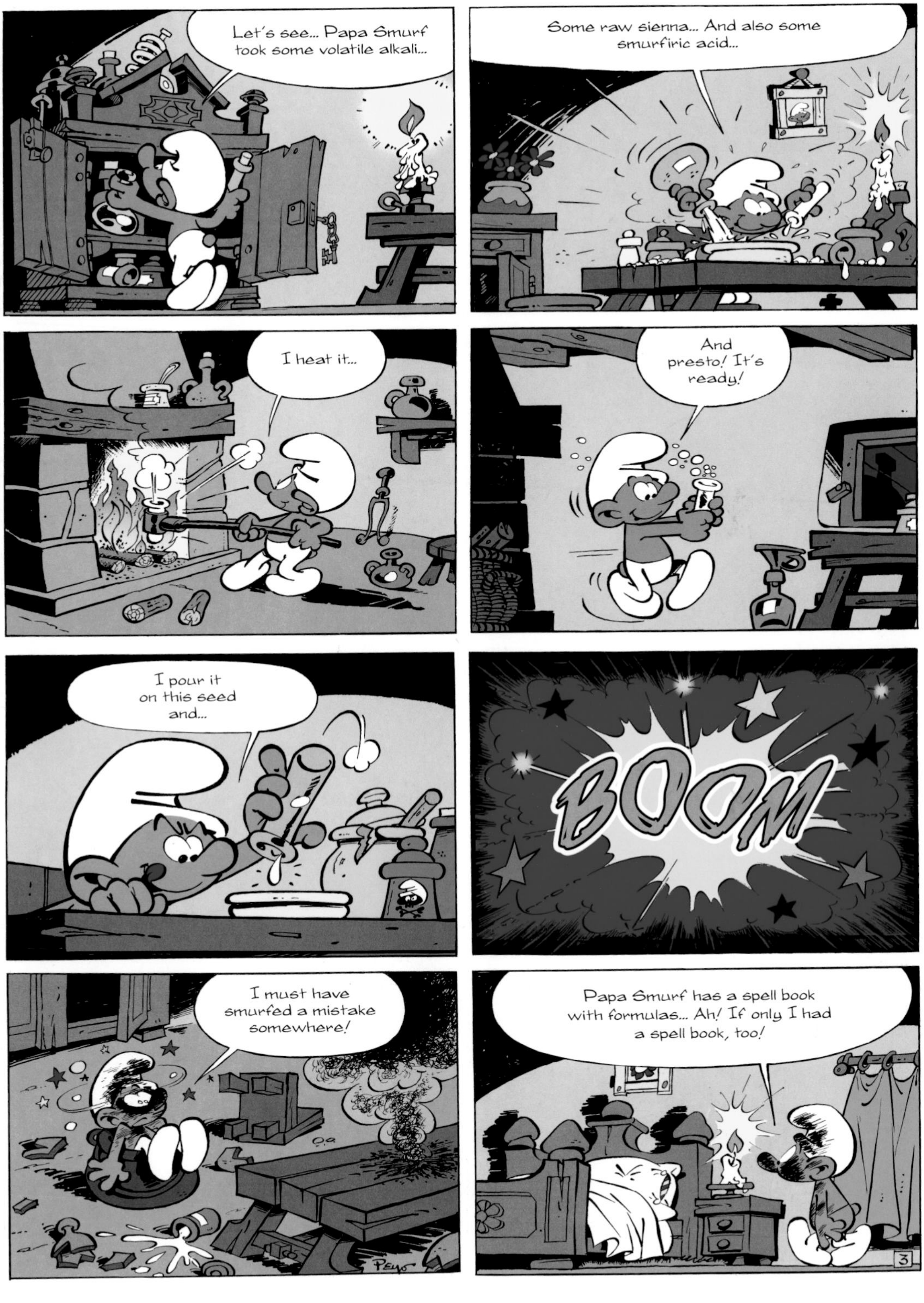
Let's see... Papa Smurf took some volatile alkali...
Some raw sienna... And also some smurfiric acid...
I heat it...
And presto! It's ready!
I pour it on this seed and...
BOOM
I must have smurfed a mistake somewhere!
PEYO
Papa Smurf has a spell book with formulas... Ah! If only I had a spell book, too!
3

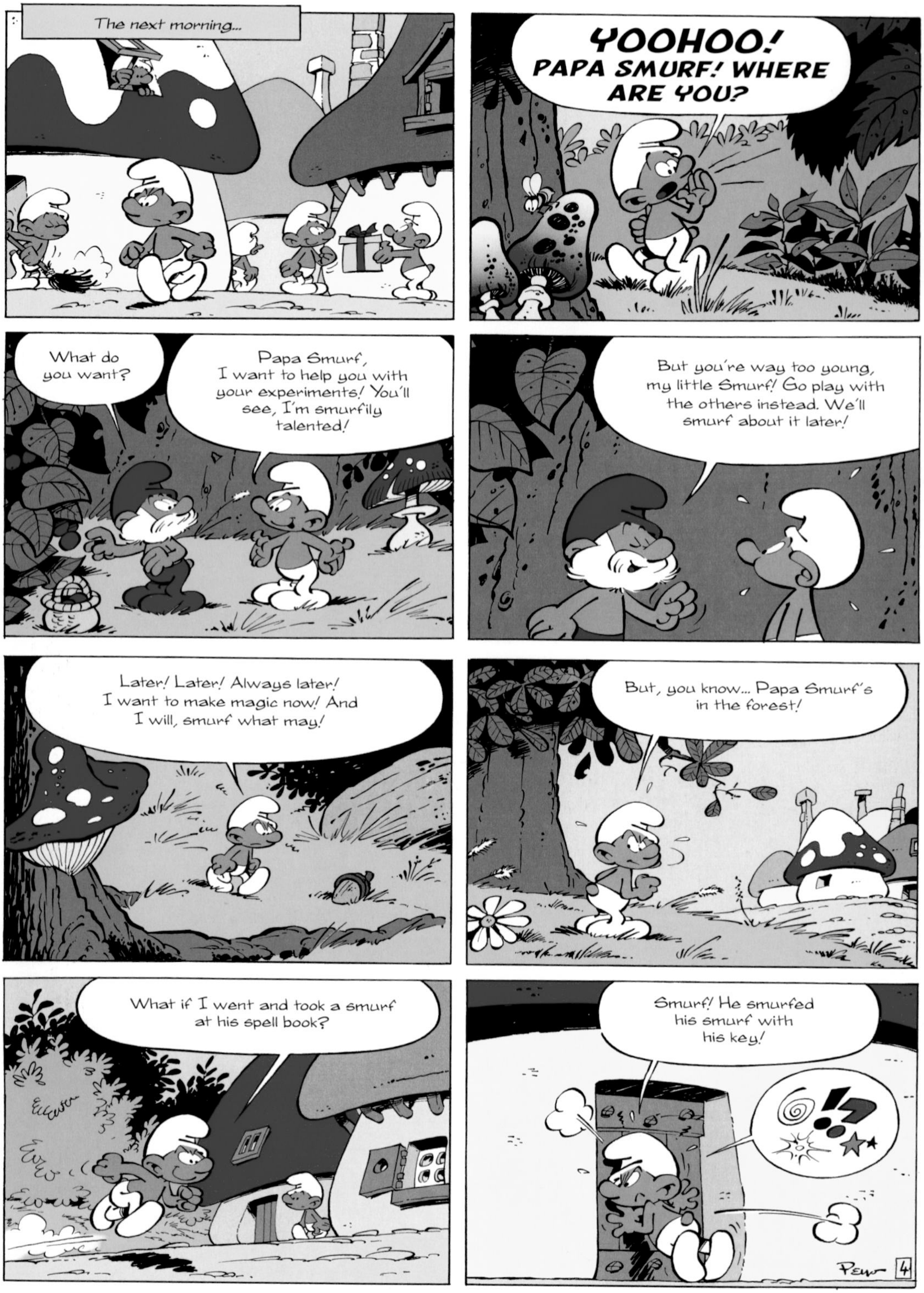
The next morning...
YOOHOO! PAPA SMURF! WHERE ARE YOU?
What do you want?
Papa Smurf, I want to help you with your experiments! You'll see, I'm smurfily talented!
But you're way too young, my little Smurf! Go play with the others instead. We'll smurf about it later!
Later! Later! Always later! I want to make magic now! And I will, smurf what may!
But, you know... Papa Smurf's in the forest!
What if I went and took a smurf at his spell book?
Smurf! He smurfed his smurf with his key!
!?
4

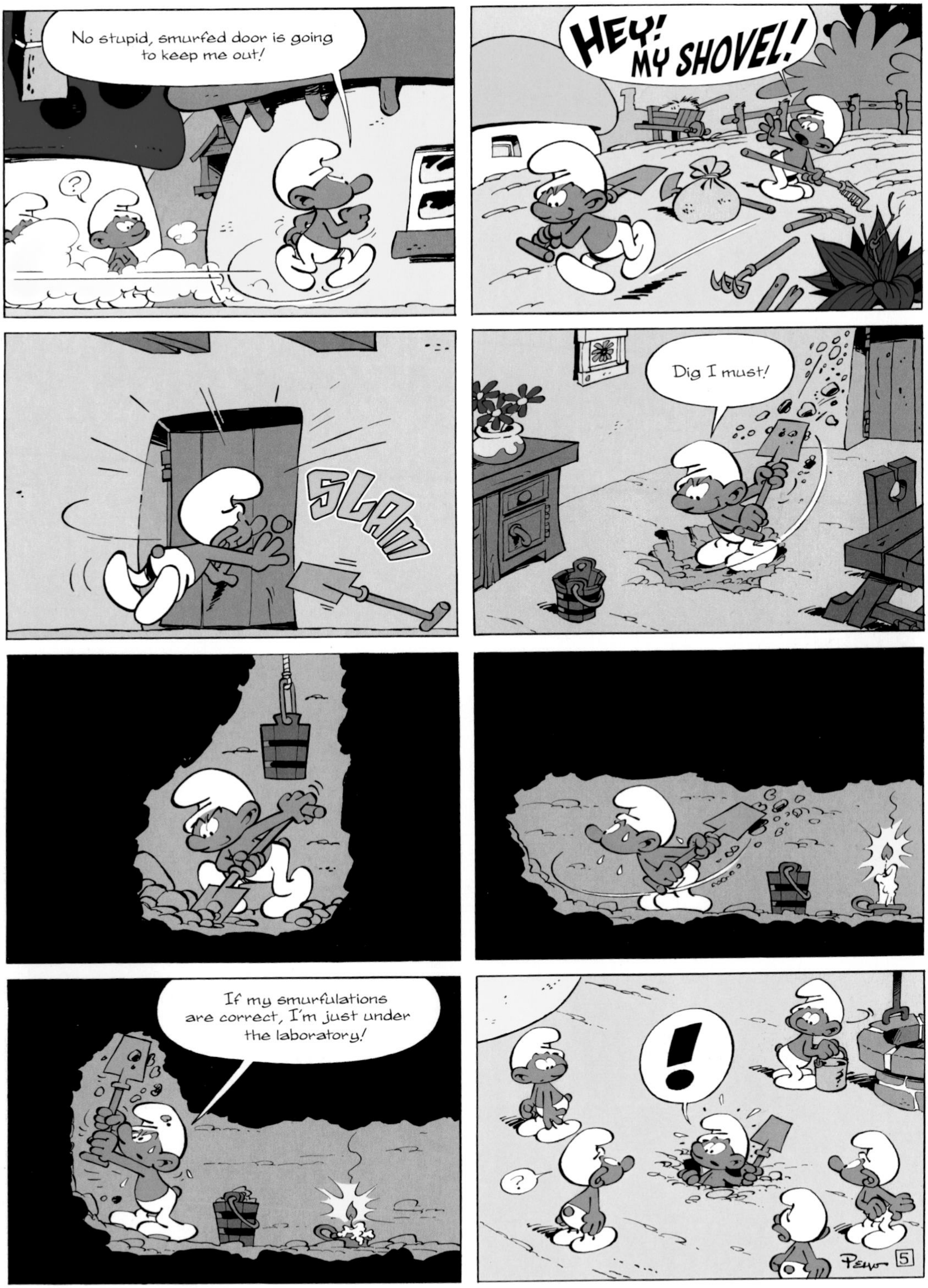
No stupid, smurfed door is going to keep me out!
?
HEY! MY SHOVEL!
SLAM
Dig I must!
If my smurfulations are correct, I'm just under the laboratory!
!
?
PEYO 5

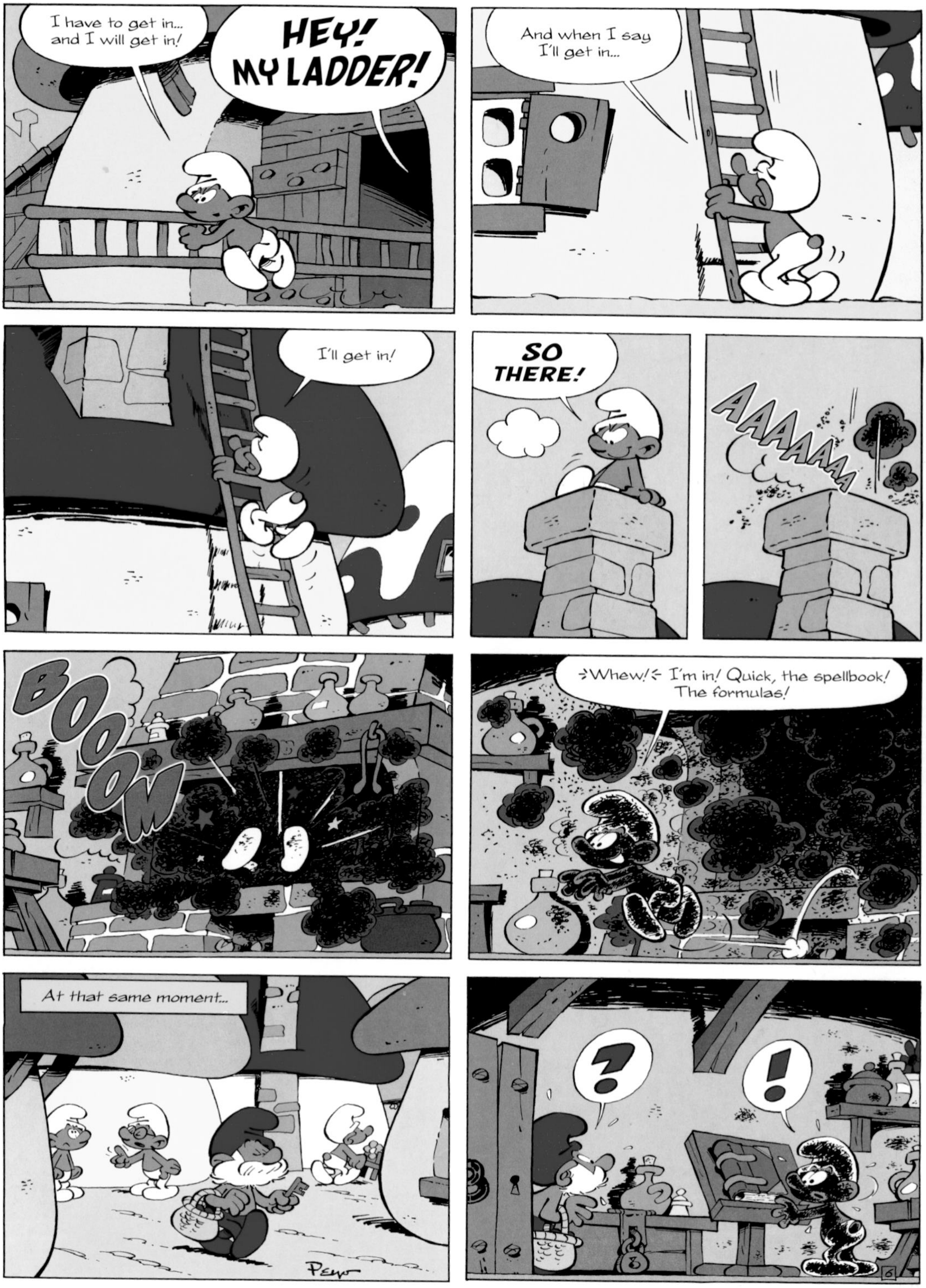
I have to get in... and I will get in!
HEY! MY LADDER!
And when I say I'll get in...
I'll get in!
SO THERE!
AAAAAAA
BOOOOM
Whew! I'm in! Quick, the spellbook! The formulas!
At that same moment...
?
!
Peyo
6

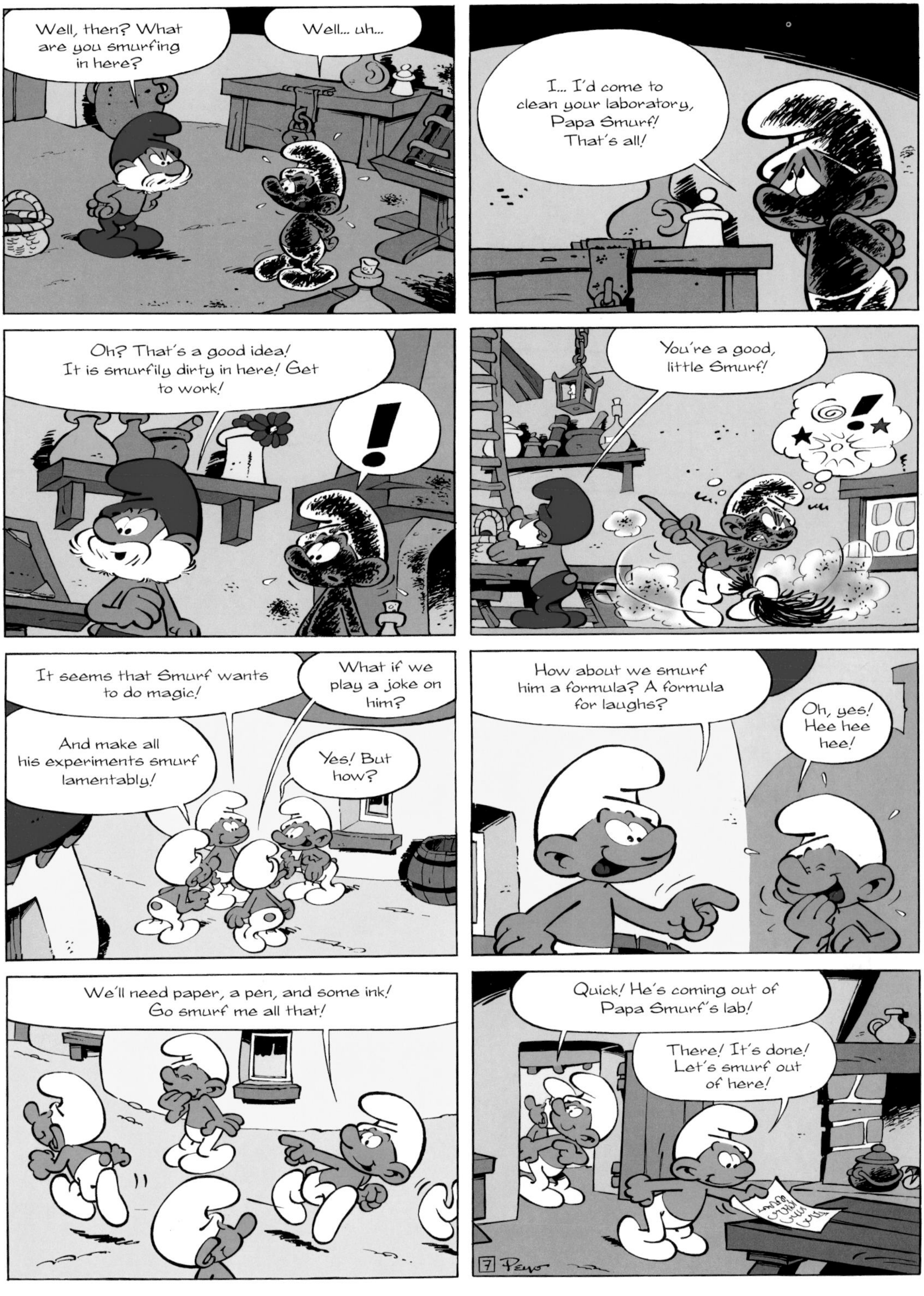
Well, then? What are you smurfing in here?
Well... uh...
I... I'd come to clean your laboratory, Papa Smurf! That's all!
Oh? That's a good idea! It is smurfily dirty in here! Get to work!
!
You're a good, little Smurf!
It seems that Smurf wants to do magic!
What if we play a joke on him?
And make all his experiments smurf lamentably!
Yes! But how?
How about we smurf him a formula? A formula for laughs?
Oh, yes! Hee hee hee!
We'll need paper, a pen, and some ink! Go smurf me all that!
Quick! He's coming out of Papa Smurf's lab!
There! It's done! Let's smurf out of here!
7 Peyo

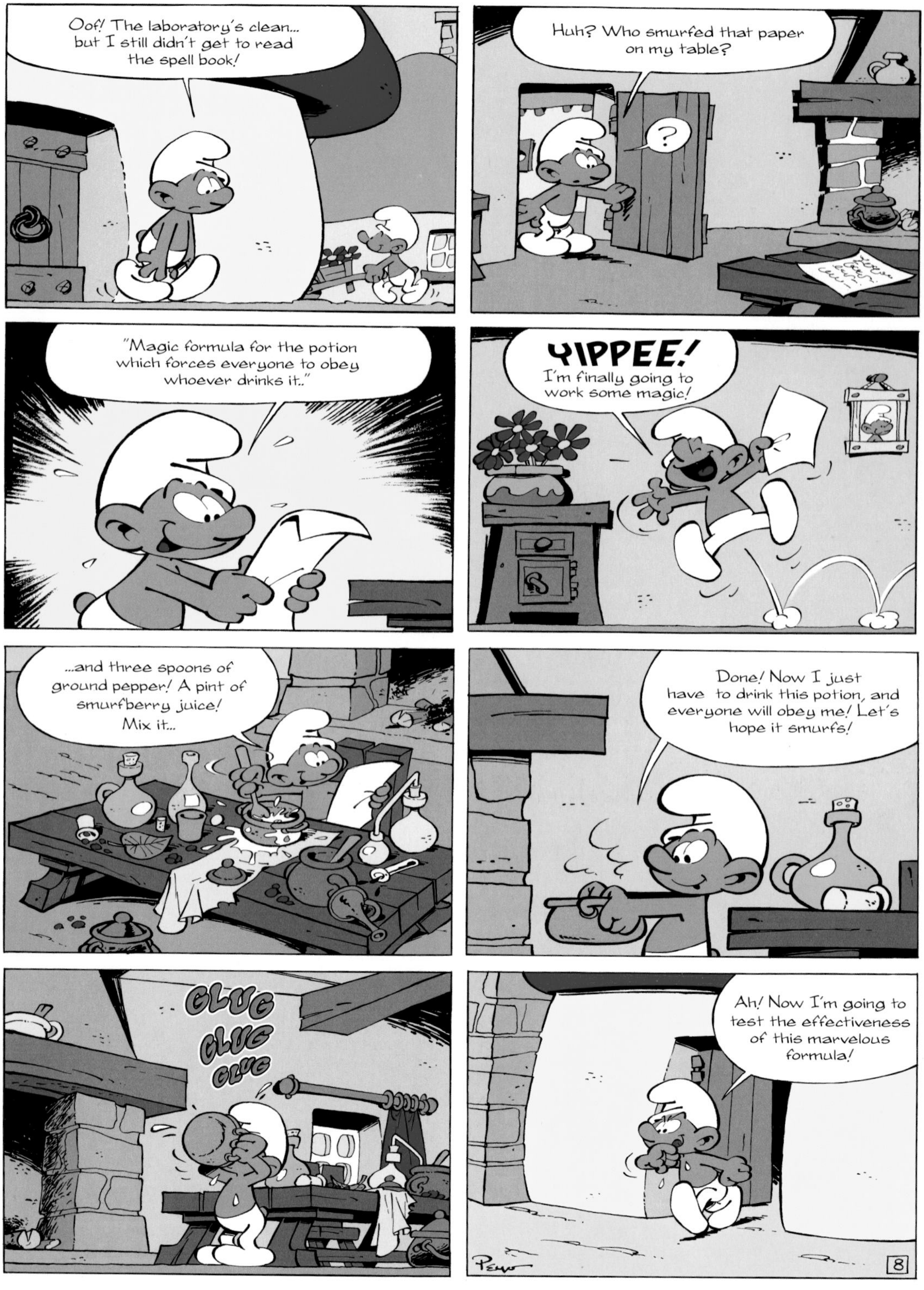

Oof! The laboratory's clean... but I still didn't get to read the spell book!
Huh? Who smurfed that paper on my table?
?
"Magic formula for the potion which forces everyone to obey whoever drinks it.."
YIPPEE!
I'm finally going to work some magic!
...and three spoons of ground pepper! A pint of smurfberry juice! Mix it...
Done! Now I just have to drink this potion, and everyone will obey me! Let's hope it smurfs!
GLUG
GLUG
GLUG
Ah! Now I'm going to test the effectiveness of this marvelous formula!
Peyo
8

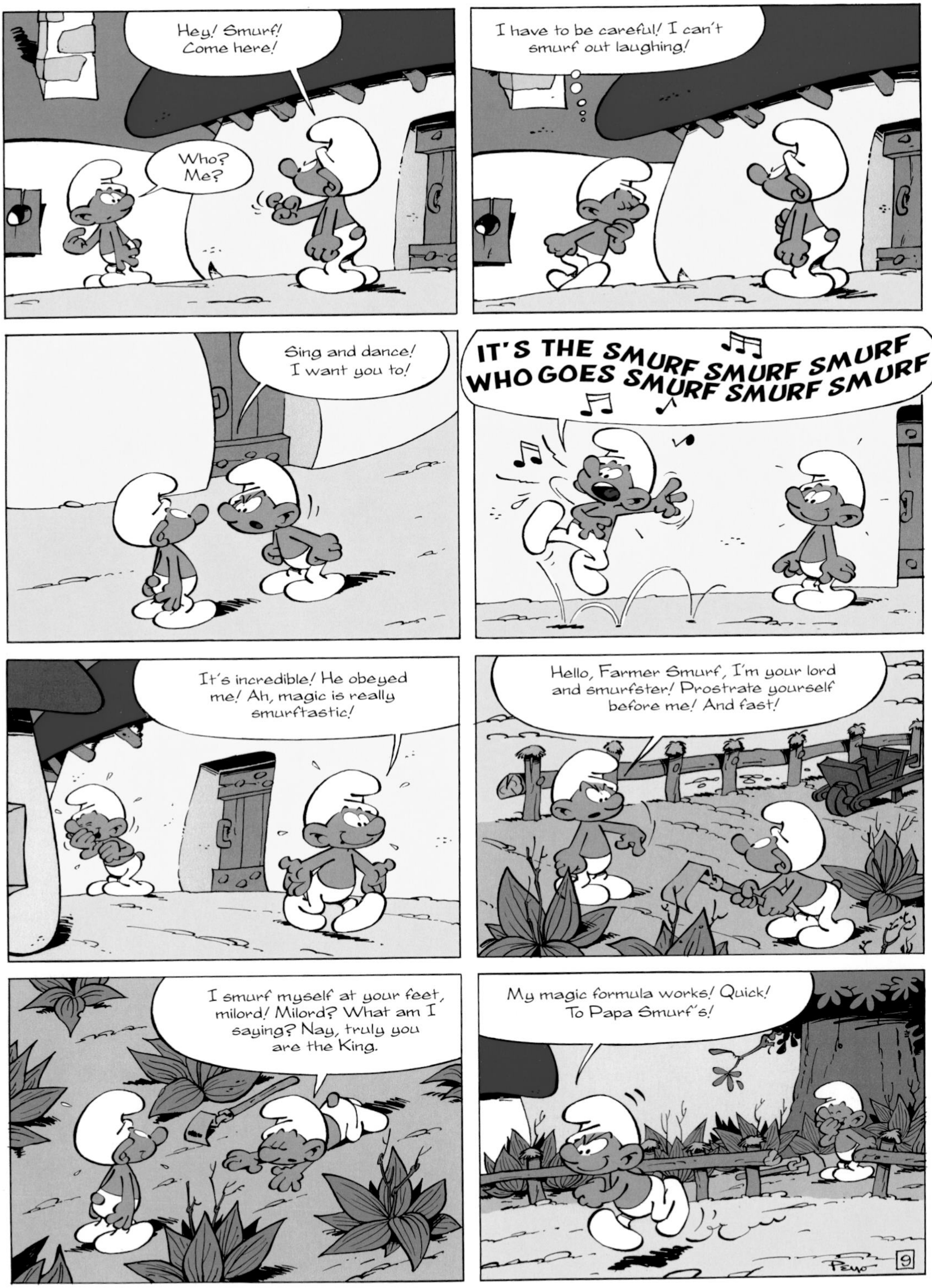
Hey! Smurf! Come here!
Who? Me?
I have to be careful! I can't smurf out laughing!
Sing and dance! I want you to!
IT'S THE SMURF SMURF SMURF WHO GOES SMURF SMURF SMURF
It's incredible! He obeyed me! Ah, magic is really smurftastic!
Hello, Farmer Smurf, I'm your lord and smurfster! Prostrate yourself before me! And fast!
I smurf myself at your feet, milord! Milord? What am I saying? Nay, truly you are the King.
My magic formula works! Quick! To Papa Smurf's!
Peyo
9

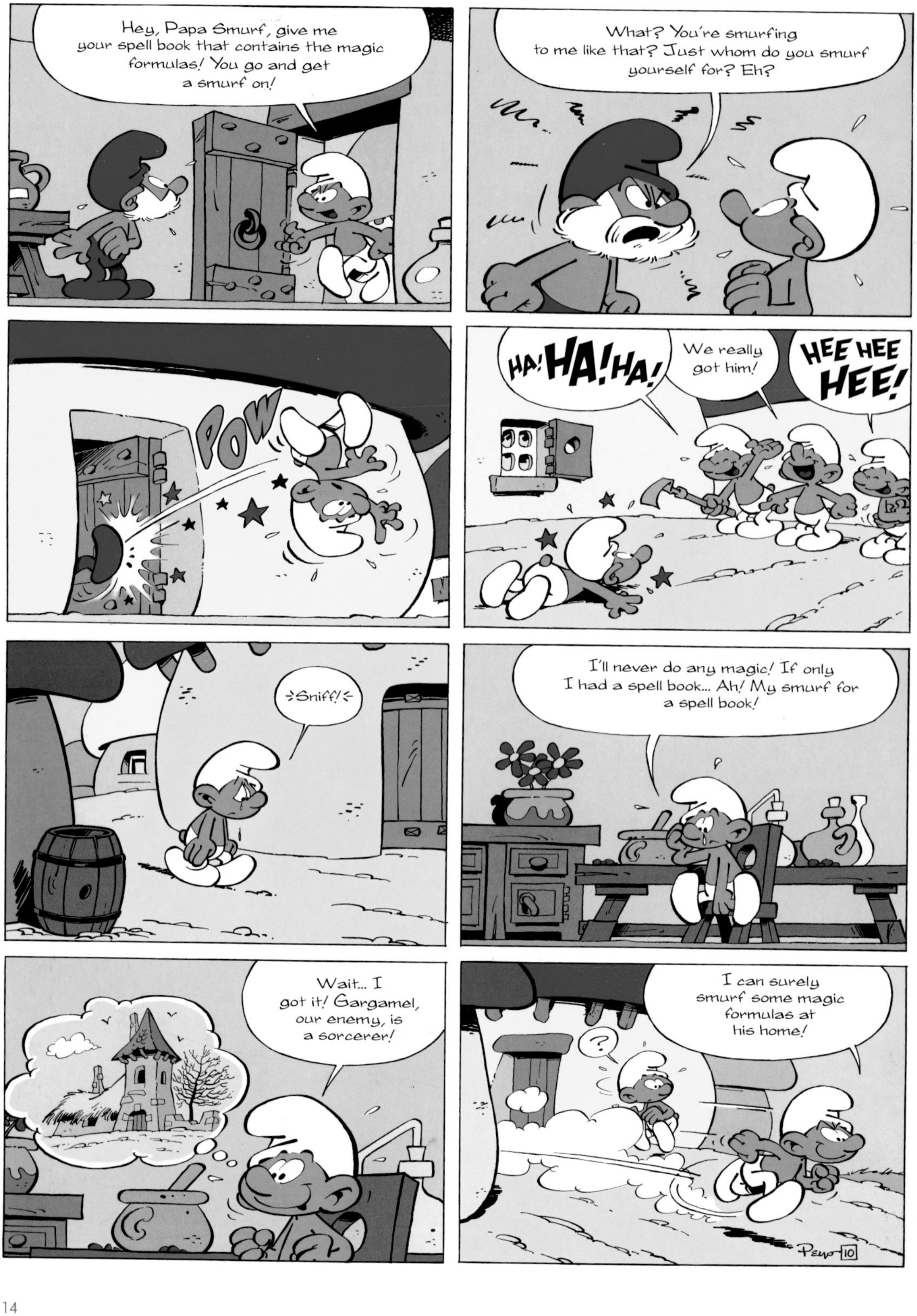
Hey, Papa Smurf, give me your spell book that contains the magic formulas! You go and get a smurf on!
What? You're smurfing to me like that? Just whom do you smurf yourself for? Eh?
POW
HA! HA! HA!
We really got him!
HEE HEE HEE!
Sniff!
I'll never do any magic! If only I had a spell book... Ah! My smurf for a spell book!
Wait... I got it! Gargamel, our enemy, is a sorcerer!
I can surely smurf some magic formulas at his home!
10

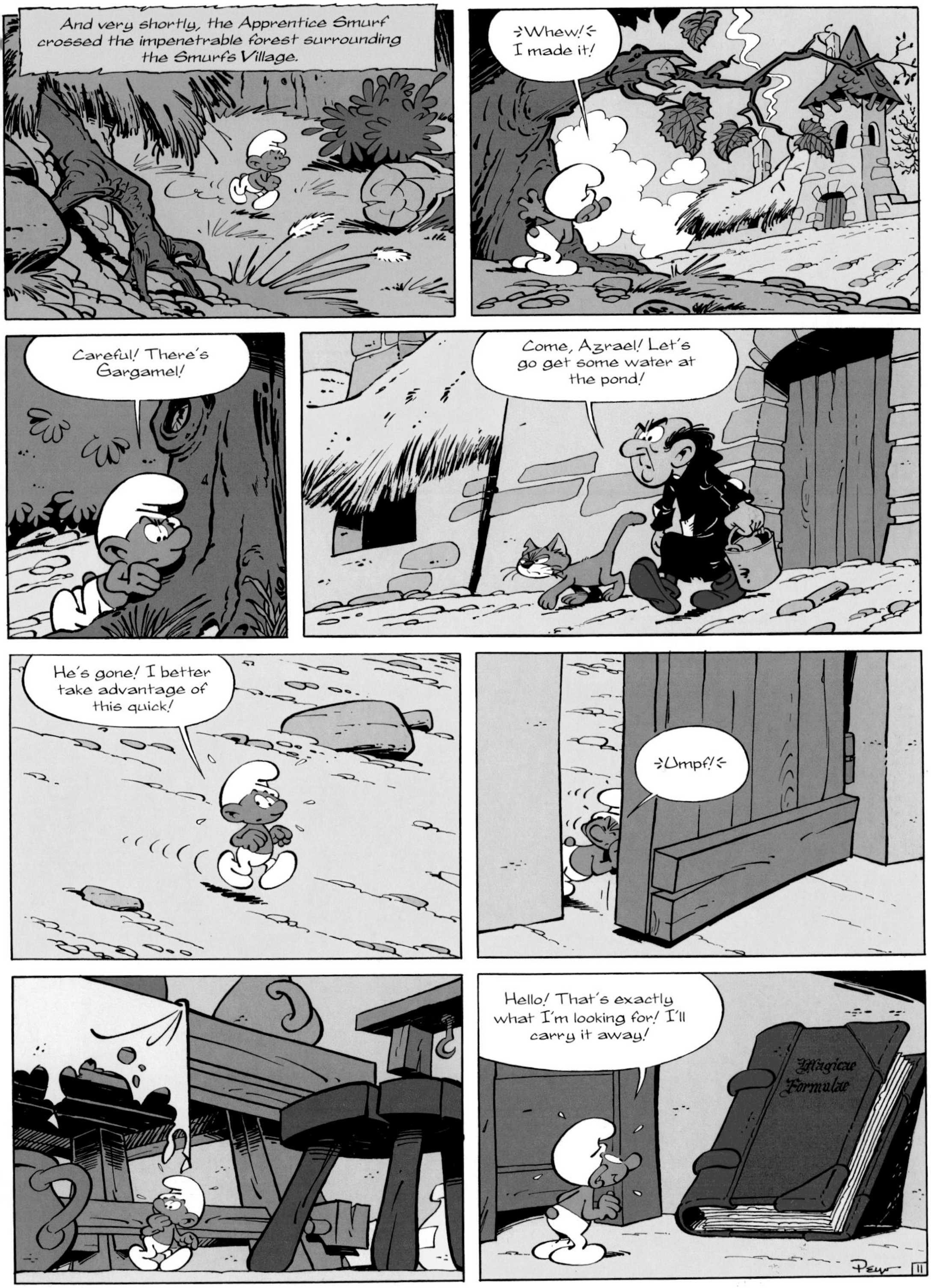
And very shortly, the Apprentice Smurf crossed the impenetrable forest surrounding the Smurfs Village.
Whew! I made it!
Careful! There's Gargamel!
Come, Azrael! Let's go get some water at the pond!
He's gone! I better take advantage of this quick!
Umpf!
Hello! That's exactly what I'm looking for! I'll carry it away!
Magicae Formulae
Peyo
11

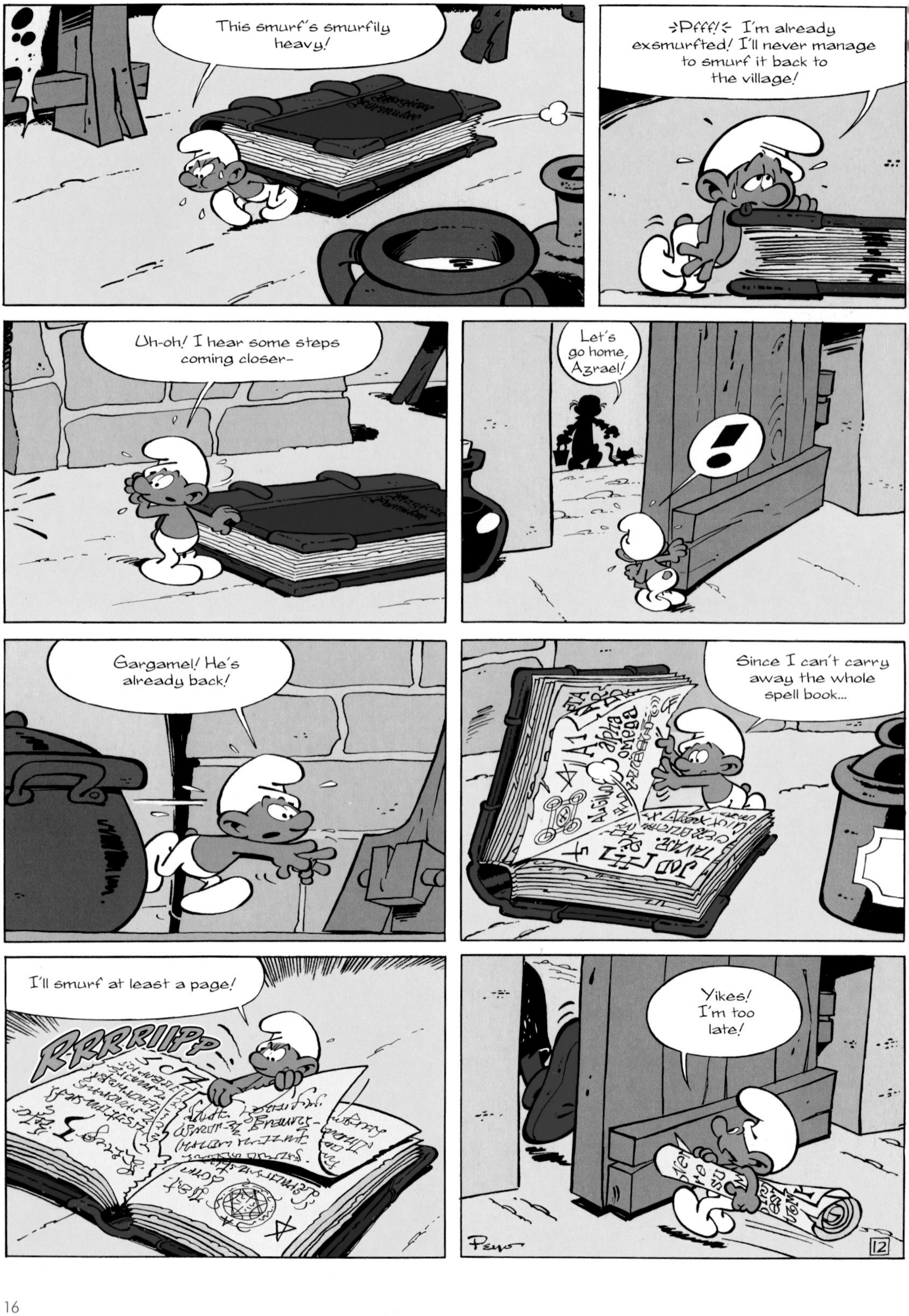
This smurf's smurfily heavy!
»Pfff!« I'm already exsmurfted! I'll never manage to smurf it back to the village!
Uh-oh! I hear some steps coming closer-
Let's go home, Azrael!
!
Gargamel! He's already back!
Since I can't carry away the whole spell book...
I'll smurf at least a page!
RRRRIIPP
Yikes! I'm too late!
Peyo
12

Quick! The window!

⌿Whew!⌿ Smurfed it!

My spell book?! What's it doing there?

Someone tore out a page! I bet it's another trick by those cursed Smurfs!

Ha ha ha! It can't be true? It's that one? Ha ha ha ha ha! They don't know what's awaiting them!

Got to hurry back home!

And a few hours later, at nightfall...

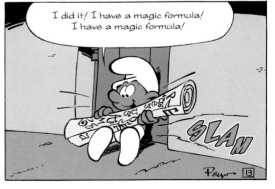

I did it! I have a magic formula! I have a magic formula!

SLAM

13

17

First smurf to do: Barricade myself in! I must keep it secret!

They'll all be comsmurfly astonished!

Let's see: **List of necessary ingredients...** Okay, I'll smurf at that later!

Preparation... hmm! None of this tells me what this spell is for!

Oh, no! The rest is on the other page... and that page is back there-- in Gargamel's book of spells!

How do I find out what this formula is for?

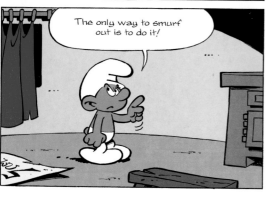

The only way to smurf out is to do it!

Let's see the ingredients first!/... Hmm... Yes... Okay... I'll go smurf all that tomorrow morning!

14

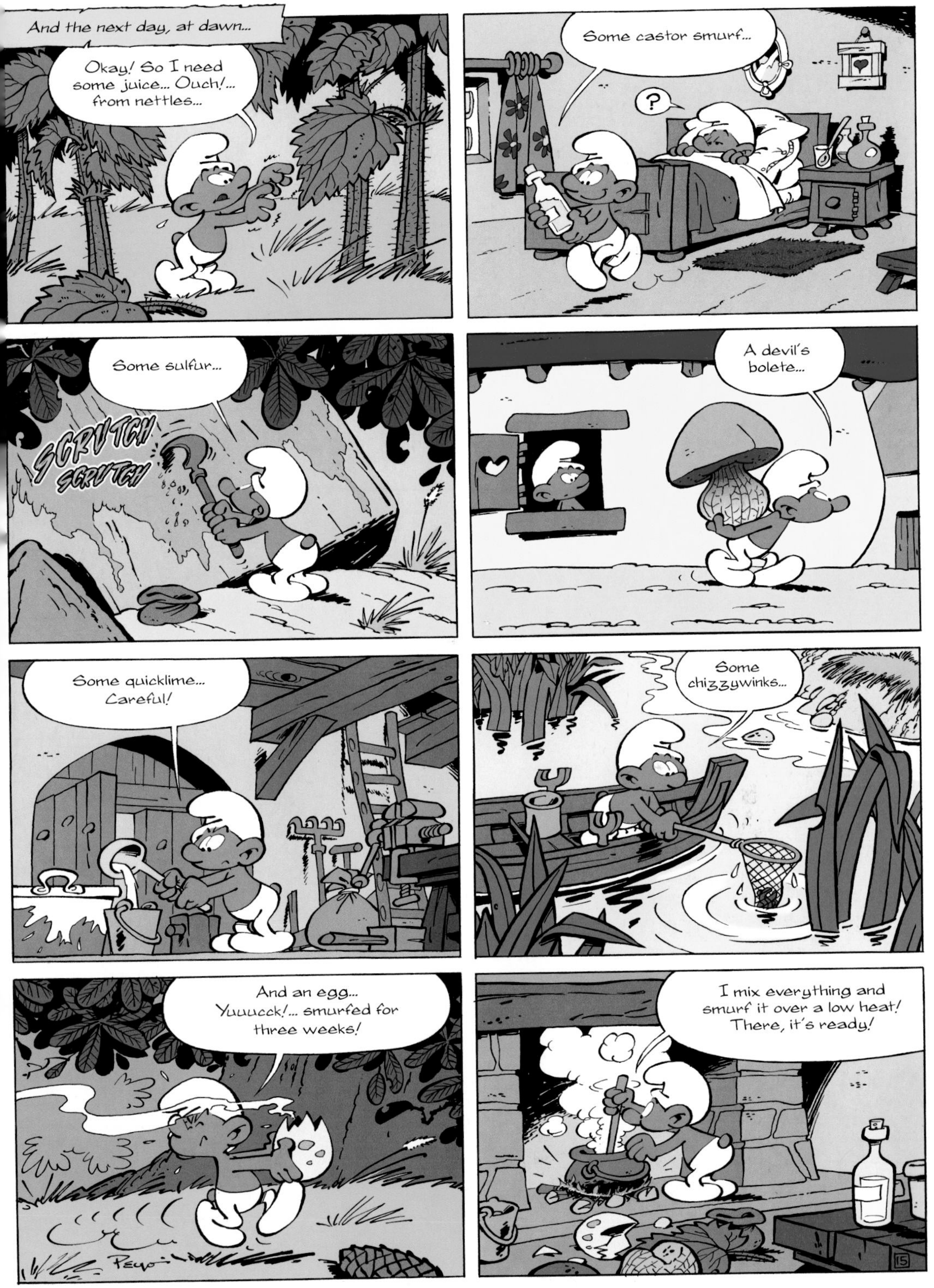
And the next day, at dawn...
Okay! So I need some juice... Ouch!... from nettles...
Some castor smurf...
?
Some sulfur...
SCRUTCH SCRUTCH
A devil's bolete...
Some quicklime... Careful!
Some chizzywinks...
And an egg... Yuuucck!... smurfed for three weeks!
I mix everything and smurf it over a low heat! There, it's ready!
Peyo
15

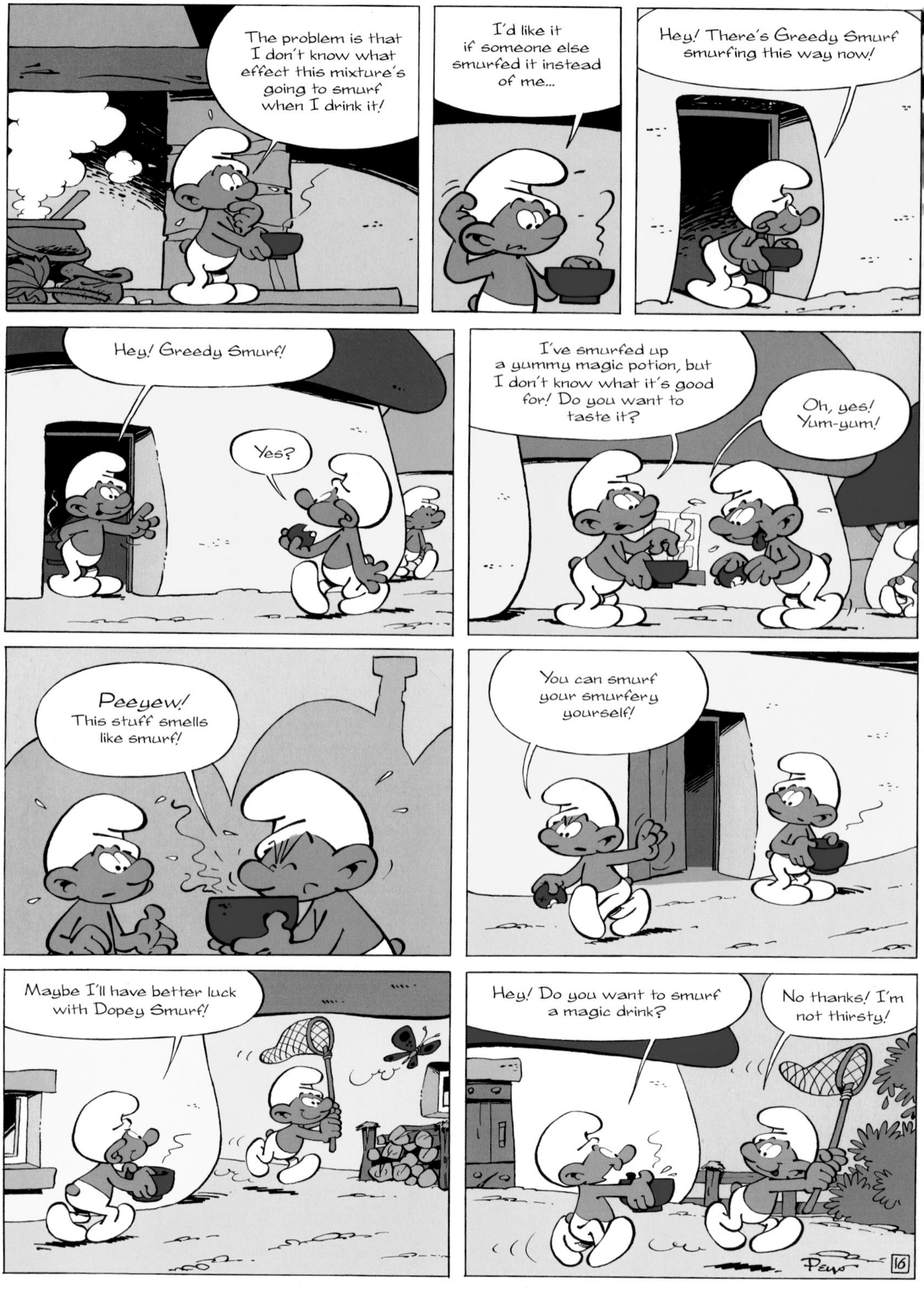
The problem is that I don't know what effect this mixture's going to smurf when I drink it!
I'd like it if someone else smurfed it instead of me...
Hey! There's Greedy Smurf smurfing this way now!
Hey! Greedy Smurf!
Yes?
I've smurfed up a yummy magic potion, but I don't know what it's good for! Do you want to taste it?
Oh, yes! Yum-yum!
Peeyew! This stuff smells like smurf!
You can smurf your smurfery yourself!
Maybe I'll have better luck with Dopey Smurf!
Hey! Do you want to smurf a magic drink?
No thanks! I'm not thirsty!
Peyo
16

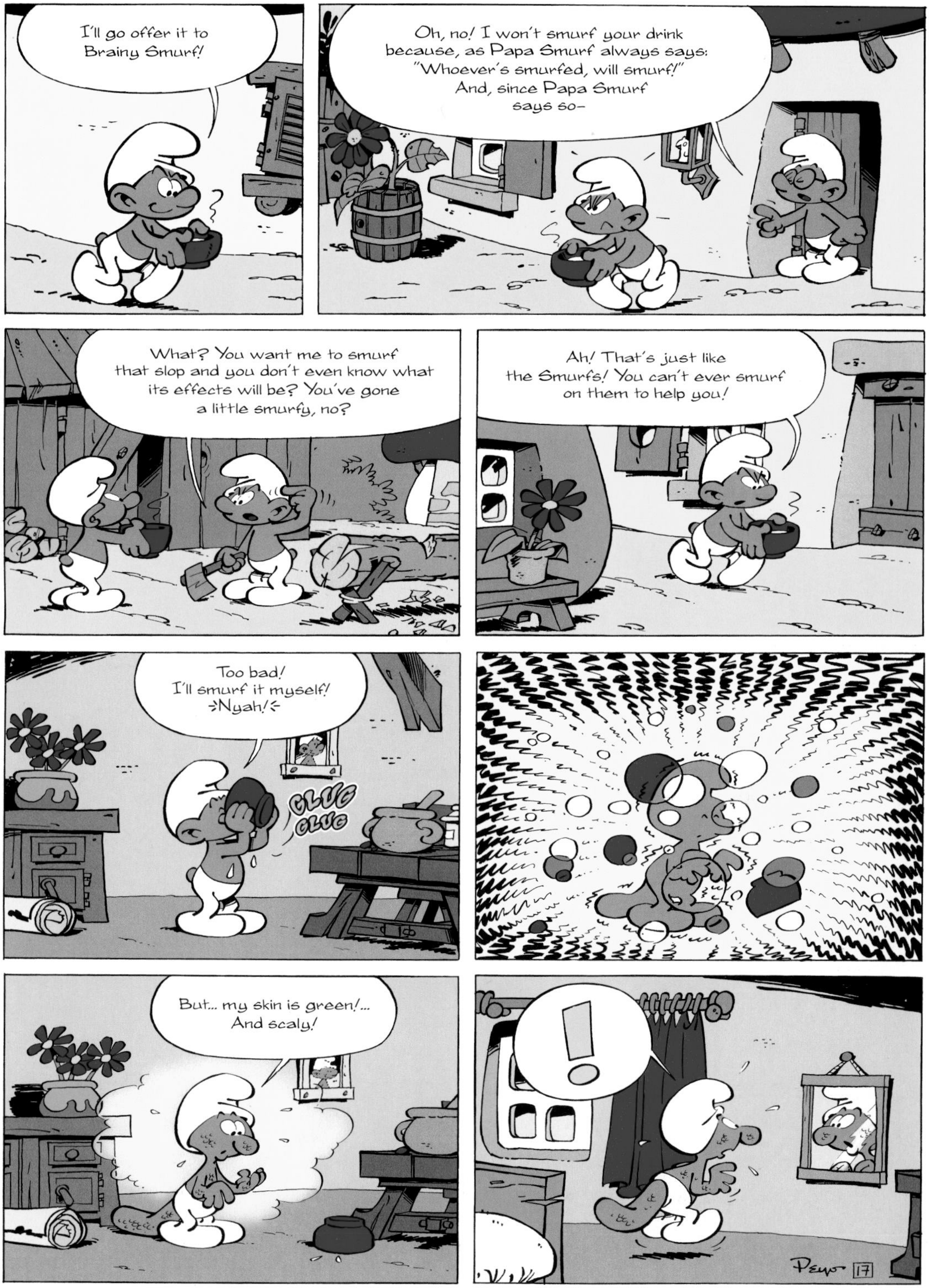

I'll go offer it to Brainy Smurf!
Oh, no! I won't smurf your drink because, as Papa Smurf always says: "Whoever's smurfed, will smurf!" And, since Papa Smurf says so–
What? You want me to smurf that slop and you don't even know what its effects will be? You've gone a little smurfy, no?
Ah! That's just like the Smurfs! You can't ever smurf on them to help you!
Too bad! I'll smurf it myself! ≯Nyah!≮
GLUG GLUG
But... my skin is green!... And scaly!
!

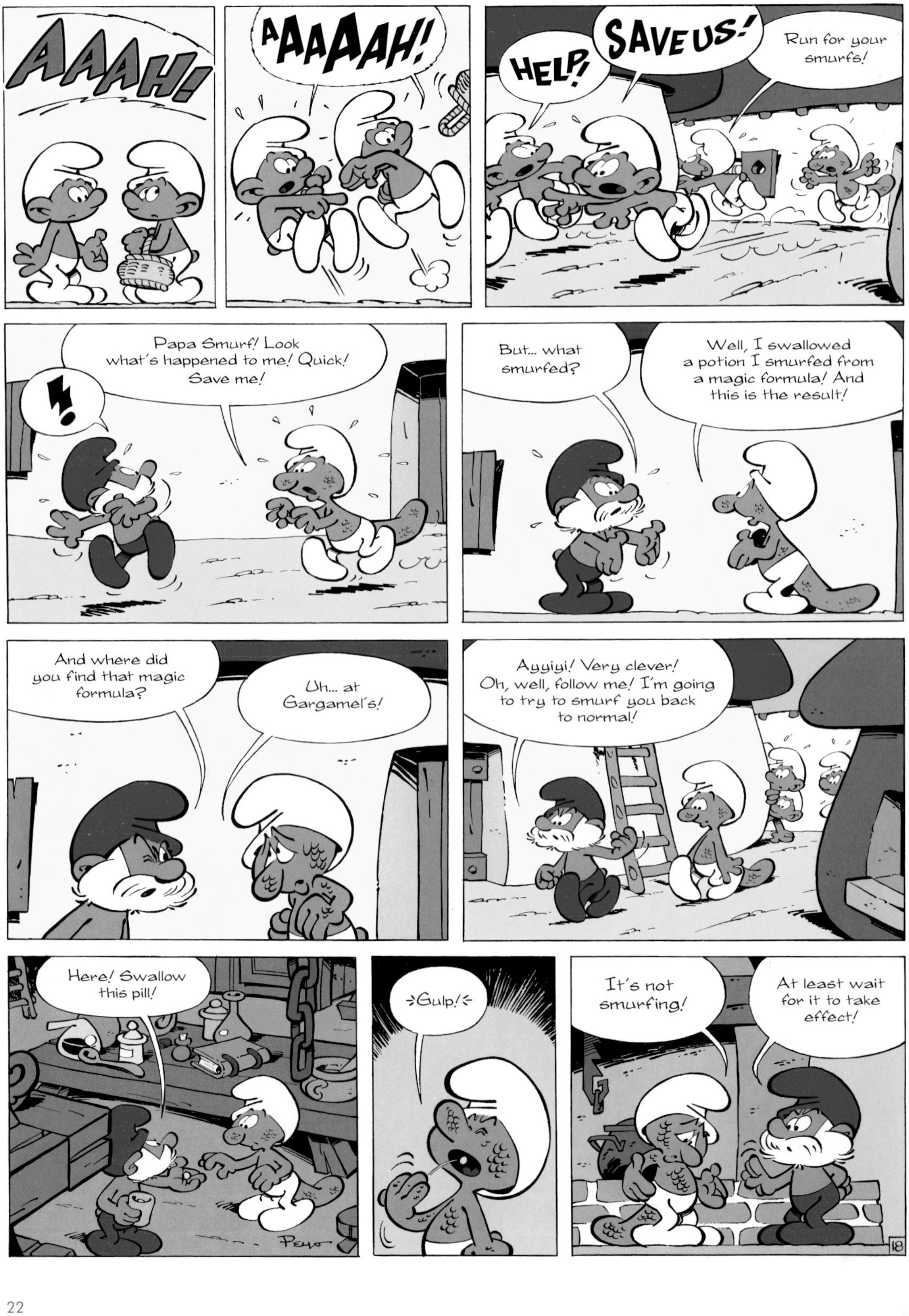
AAAH!
AAAAAH!
HELP!
SAVE US!
Run for your smurfs!
Papa Smurf! Look what's happened to me! Quick! Save me!
!
But... what smurfed?
Well, I swallowed a potion I smurfed from a magic formula! And this is the result!
And where did you find that magic formula?
Uh... at Gargamel's!
Ayyiyi! Very clever! Oh, well, follow me! I'm going to try to smurf you back to normal!
Here! Swallow this pill!
PEYO
Gulp!
It's not smurfing!
At least wait for it to take effect!
18

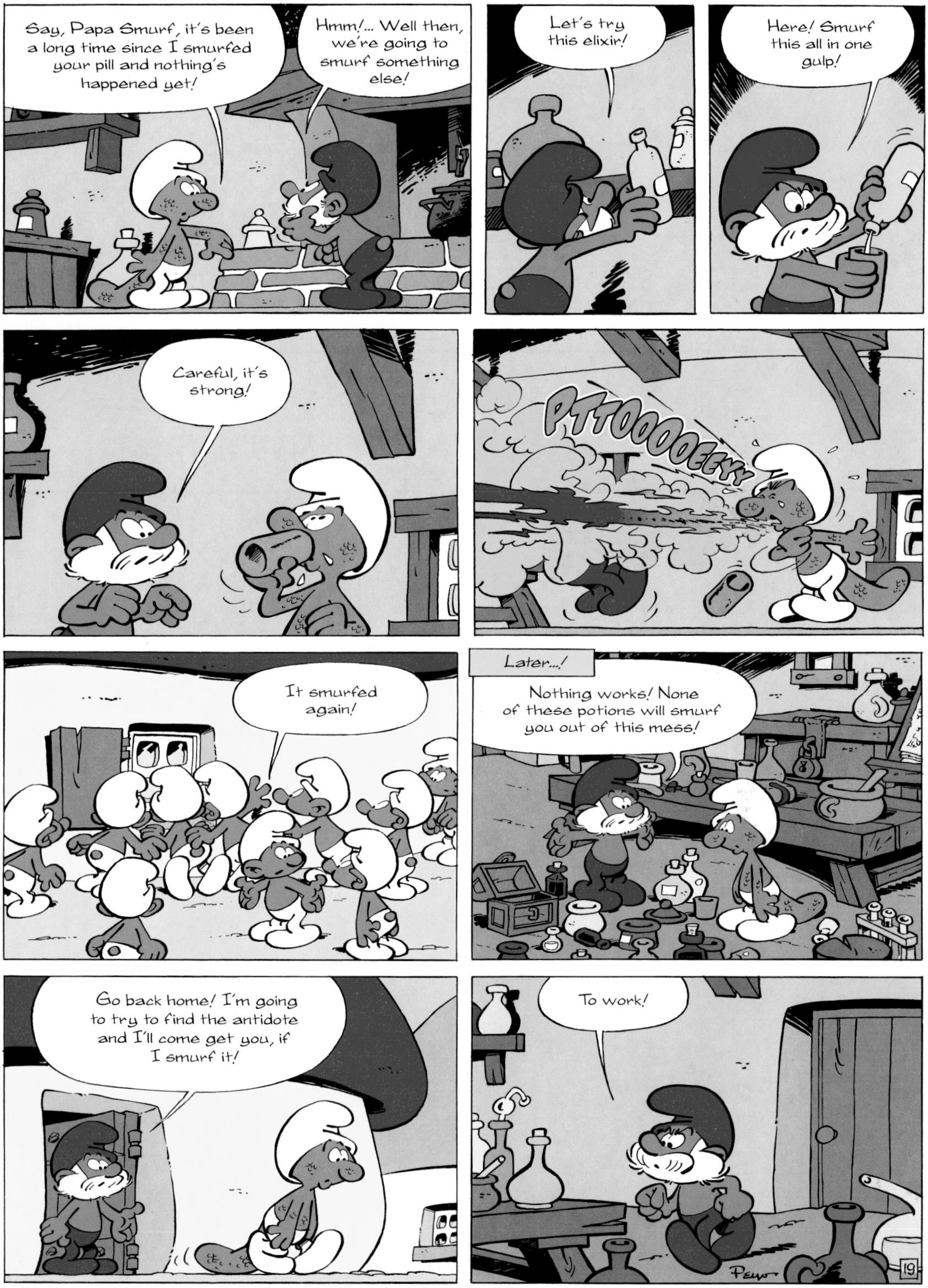
Say, Papa Smurf, it's been a long time since I smurfed your pill and nothing's happened yet!
Hmm!... Well then, we're going to smurf something else!
Let's try this elixir!
Here! Smurf this all in one gulp!
Careful, it's strong!
PTTOOOOOEEYY
It smurfed again!
Later...!
Nothing works! None of these potions will smurf you out of this mess!
Go back home! I'm going to try to find the antidote and I'll come get you, if I smurf it!
To work!
19
Peyo

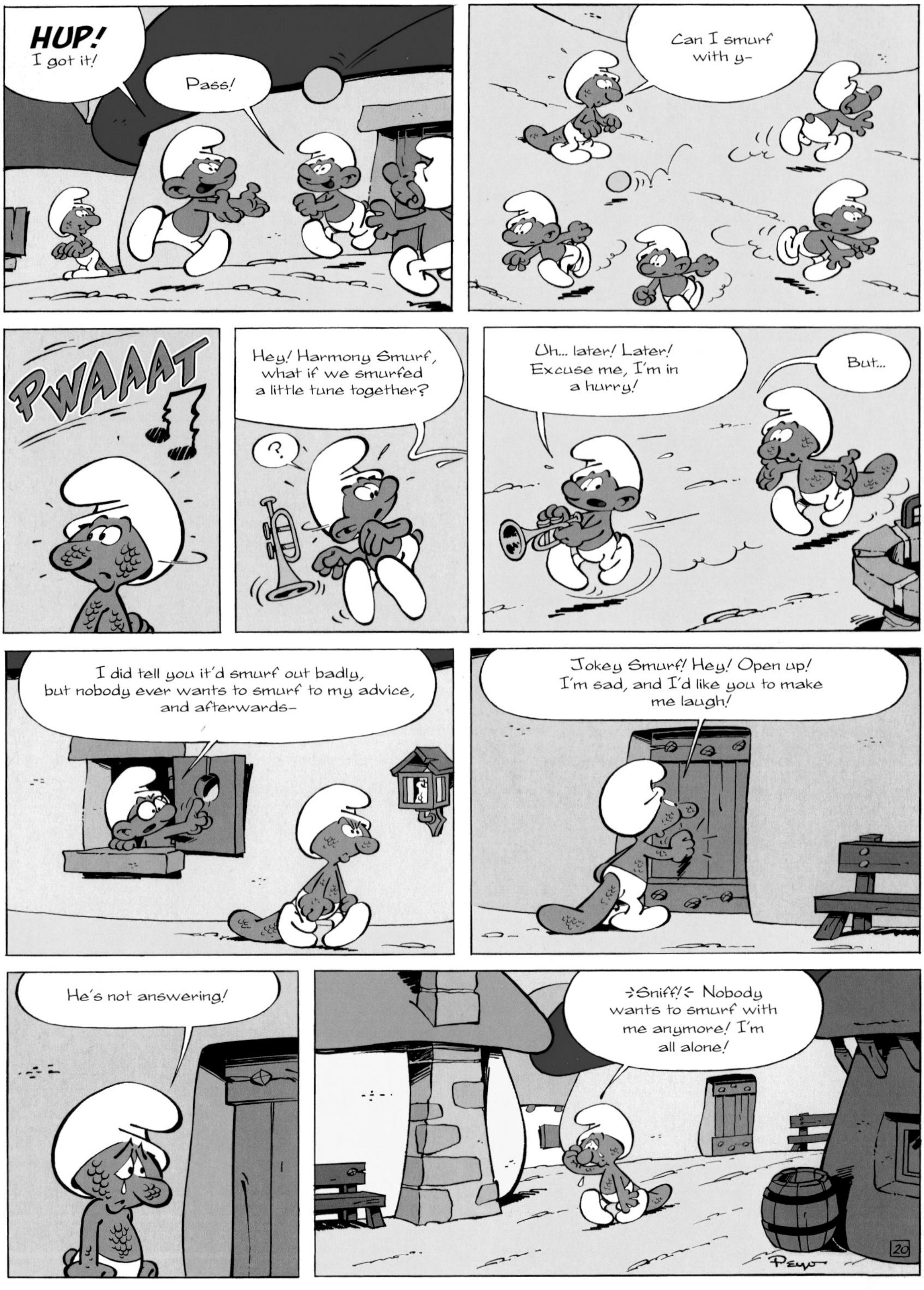
HUP! I got it!
Pass!
Can I smurf with y–
PWAAAT
Hey! Harmony Smurf, what if we smurfed a little tune together?
?
Uh... later! Later! Excuse me, I'm in a hurry!
But...
I did tell you it'd smurf out badly, but nobody ever wants to smurf to my advice, and afterwards–
Jokey Smurf! Hey! Open up! I'm sad, and I'd like you to make me laugh!
He's not answering!
Sniff! Nobody wants to smurf with me anymore! I'm all alone!
20
Peyo

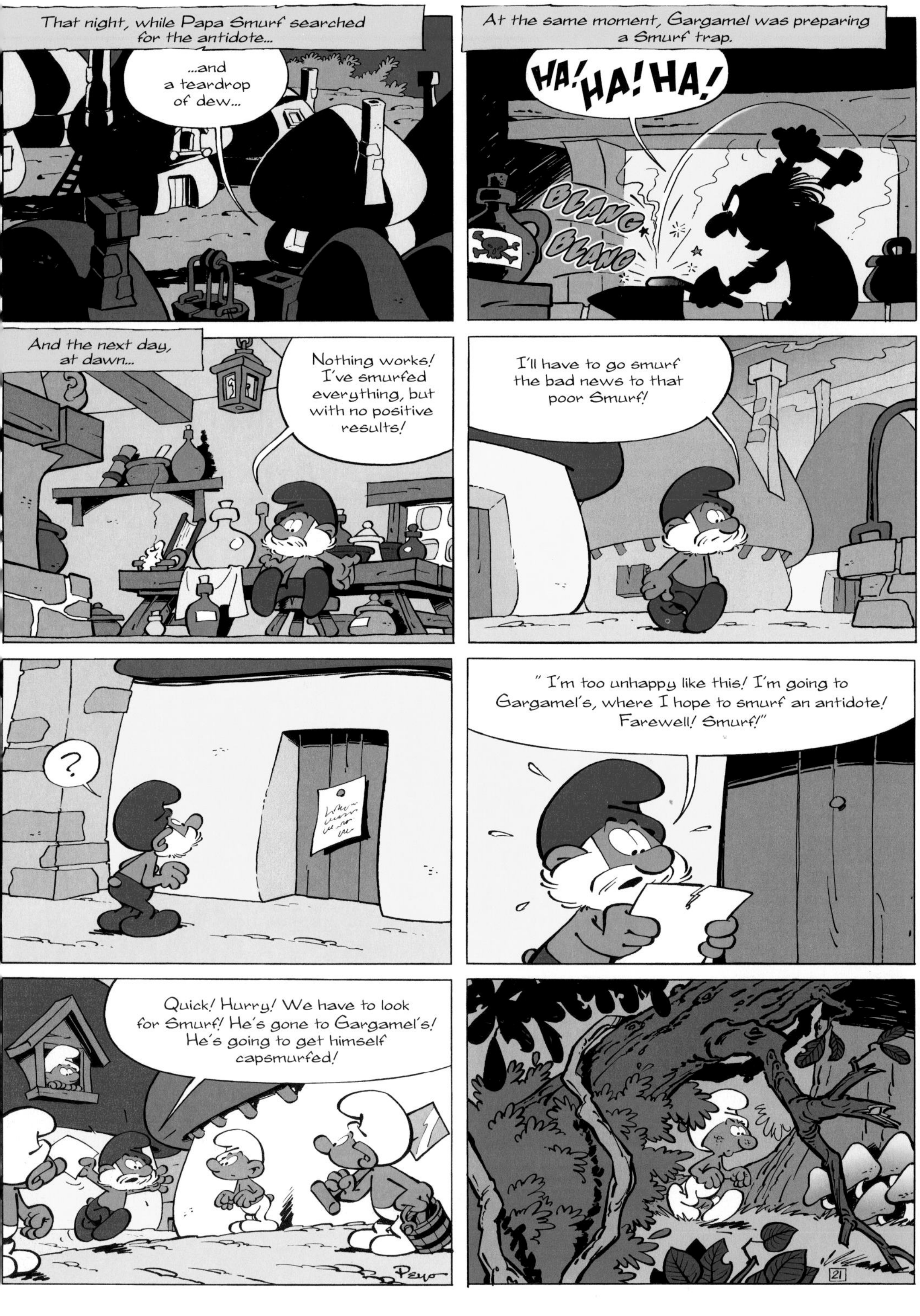
That night, while Papa Smurf searched for the antidote...
...and a teardrop of dew...
At the same moment, Gargamel was preparing a Smurf trap.
HA! HA! HA!
BLANG BLANG
And the next day, at dawn...
Nothing works! I've smurfed everything, but with no positive results!
I'll have to go smurf the bad news to that poor Smurf!
?
" I'm too unhappy like this! I'm going to Gargamel's, where I hope to smurf an antidote! Farewell! Smurf!"
Quick! Hurry! We have to look for Smurf! He's gone to Gargamel's! He's going to get himself capsmurfed!
Peyo
21

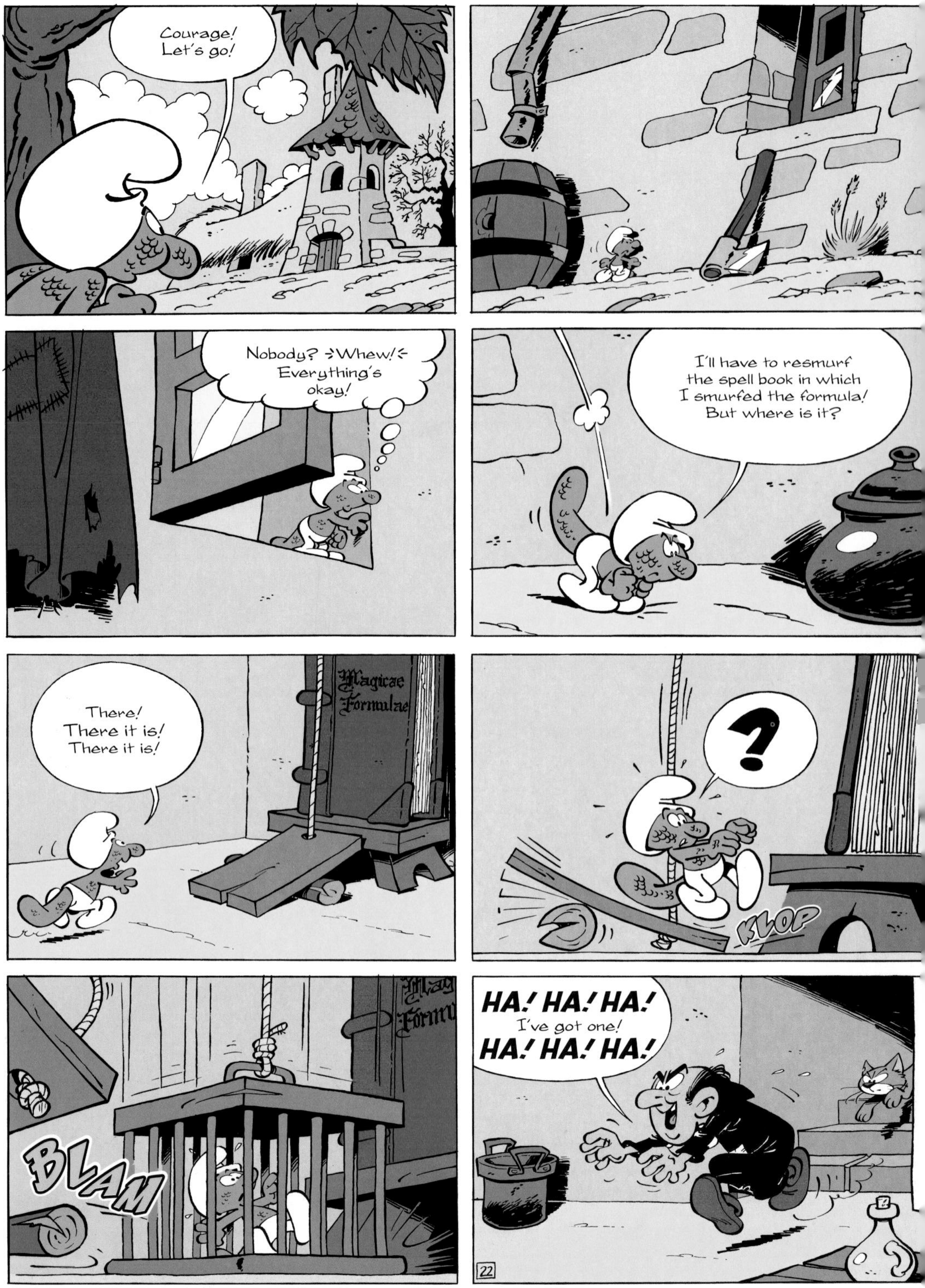
Courage! Let's go!
Nobody? Whew! Everything's okay!
I'll have to resmurf the spell book in which I smurfed the formula! But where is it?
There! There it is! There it is!
Magicae Formulae
?
KLOP
BLAM
HA! HA! HA! I've got one! HA! HA! HA!
22

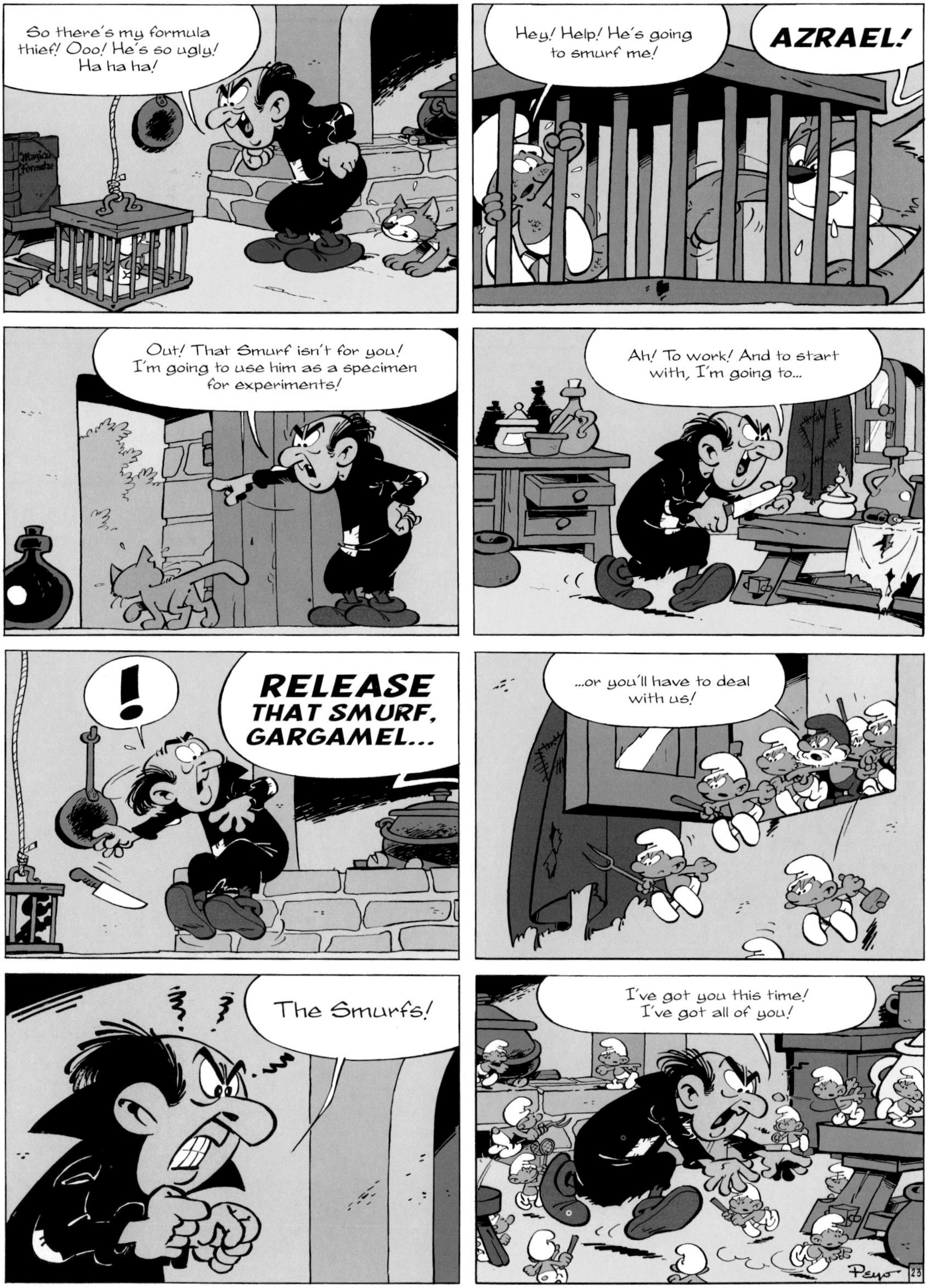
So there's my formula thief! Ooo! He's so ugly! Ha ha ha!
Magical Formulae
Hey! Help! He's going to smurf me!
AZRAEL!
Out! That Smurf isn't for you! I'm going to use him as a specimen for experiments!
Ah! To work! And to start with, I'm going to...
!
RELEASE THAT SMURF, GARGAMEL...
...or you'll have to deal with us!
The Smurfs!
I've got you this time! I've got all of you!
23

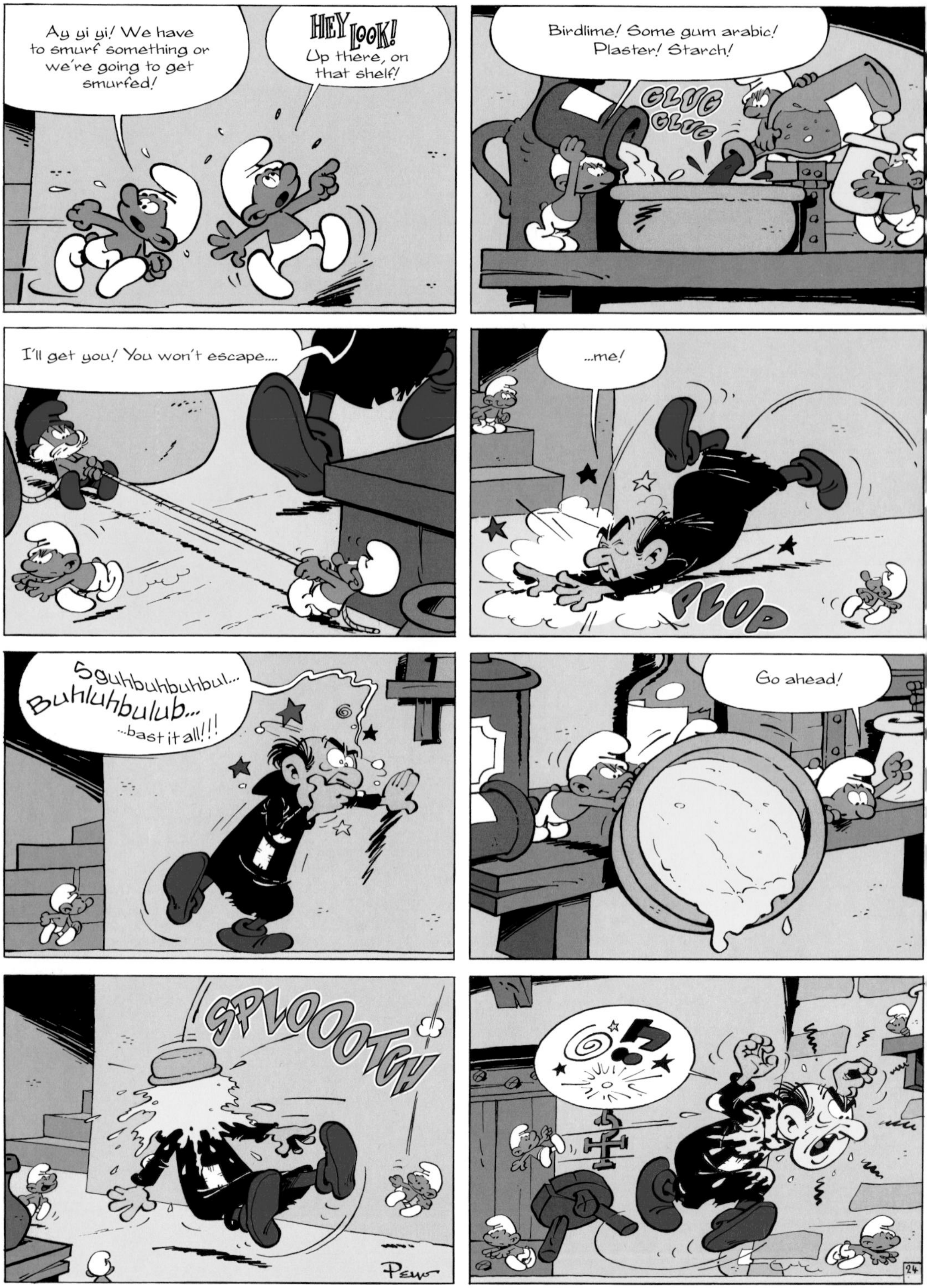
Ay yi yi! We have to smurf something or we're going to get smurfed!
HEY LOOK! Up there, on that shelf!
Birdlime! Some gum arabic! Plaster! Starch!
GLUG GLUG
I'll get you! You won't escape....
...me!
PLOP
Sguhbuhbuhbul... Buhluhbulub... ...bast it all!!!
Go ahead!
SPLOOOOTCH
Peyo
24

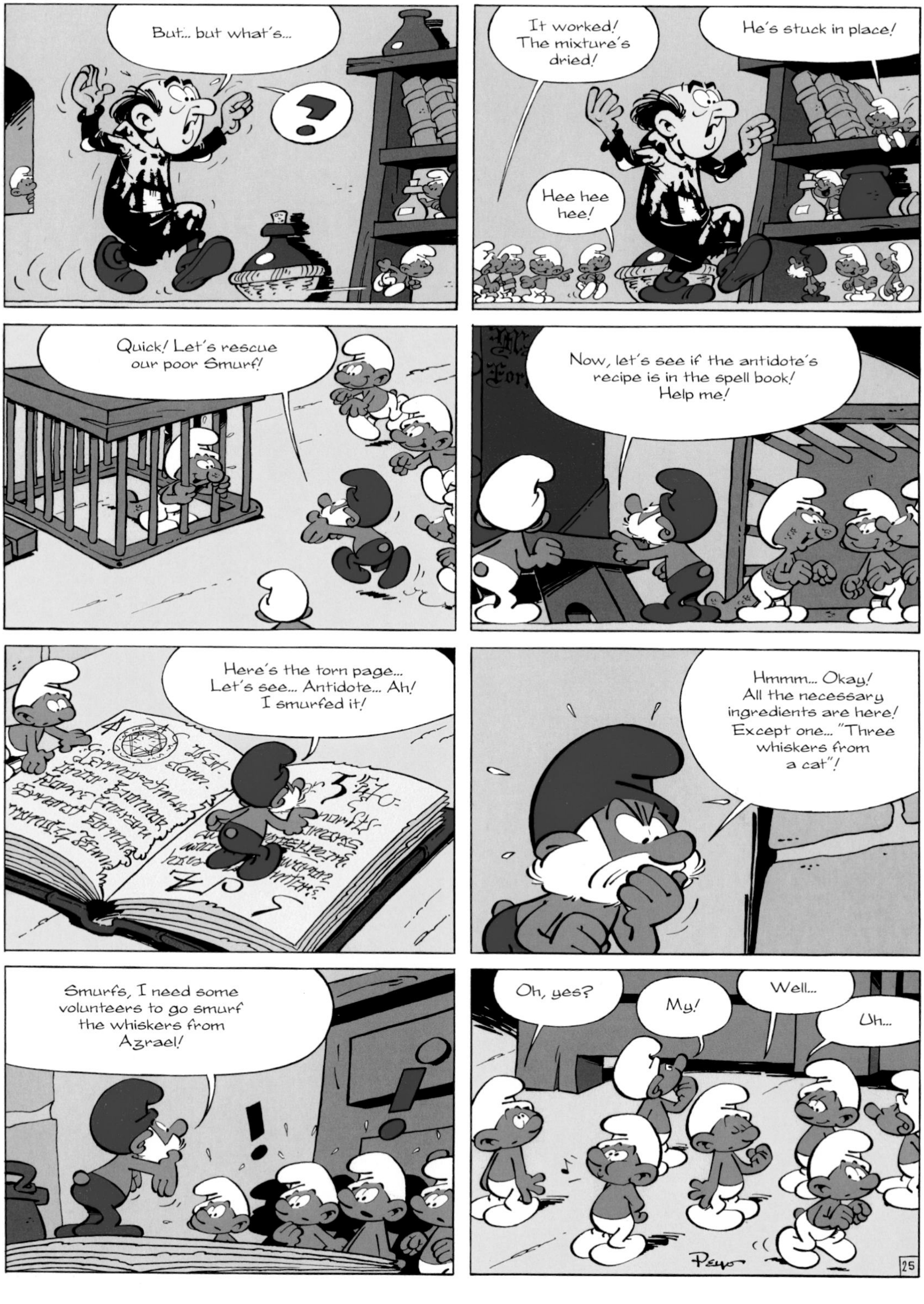
But... but what's...
?
It worked! The mixture's dried!
He's stuck in place!
Hee hee hee!
Quick! Let's rescue our poor Smurf!
Now, let's see if the antidote's recipe is in the spell book! Help me!
Here's the torn page... Let's see... Antidote... Ah! I smurfed it!
Hmmm... Okay! All the necessary ingredients are here! Except one... "Three whiskers from a cat"!
Smurfs, I need some volunteers to go smurf the whiskers from Azrael!
!
Oh, yes?
My!
Well...
Uh...
Peyo
25

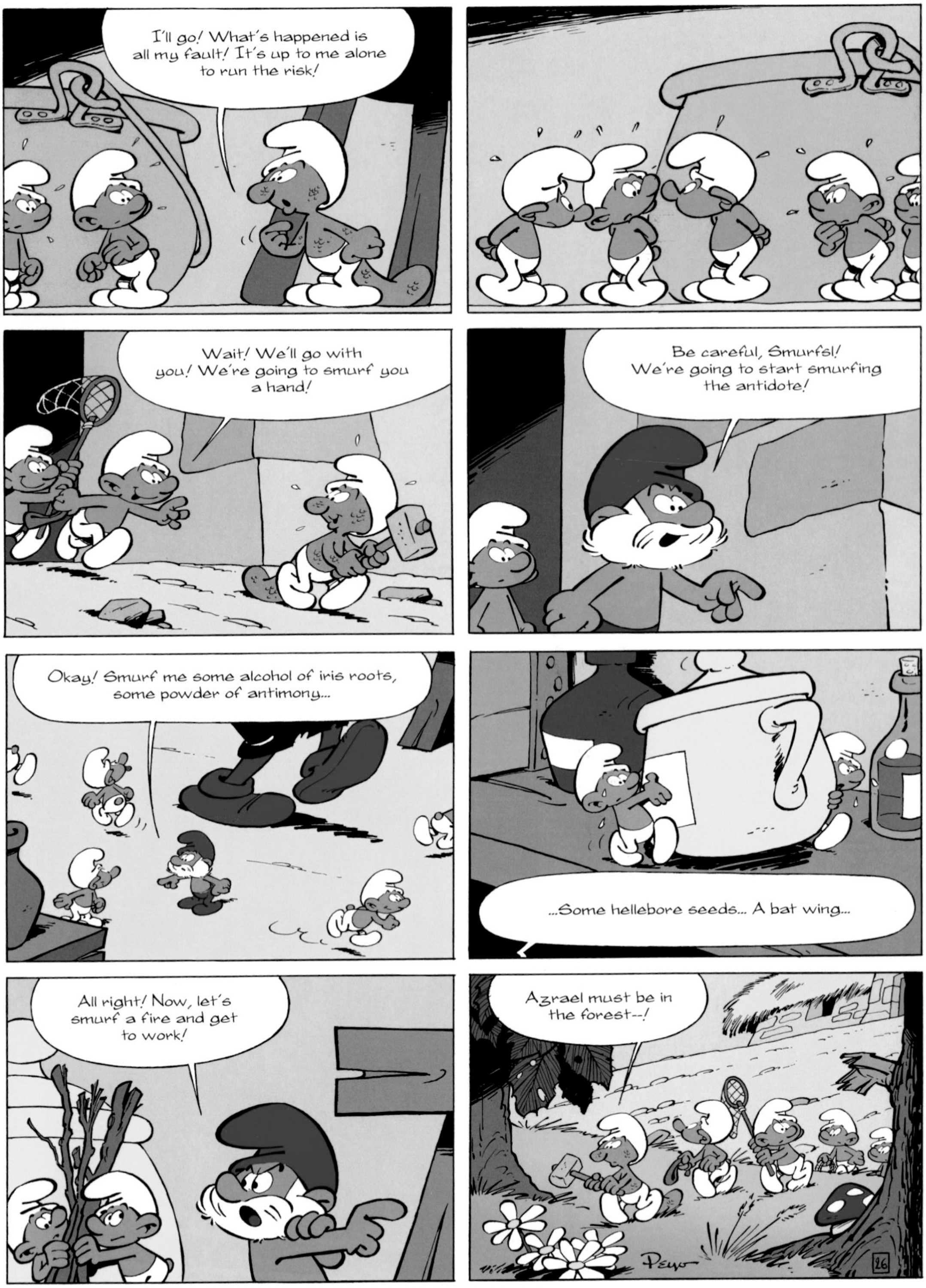
I'll go! What's happened is all my fault! It's up to me alone to run the risk!
Wait! We'll go with you! We're going to smurf you a hand!
Be careful, Smurfs!! We're going to start smurfing the antidote!
Okay! Smurf me some alcohol of iris roots, some powder of antimony...
...Some hellebore seeds... A bat wing...
All right! Now, let's smurf a fire and get to work!
Azrael must be in the forest--!
Peyo
26

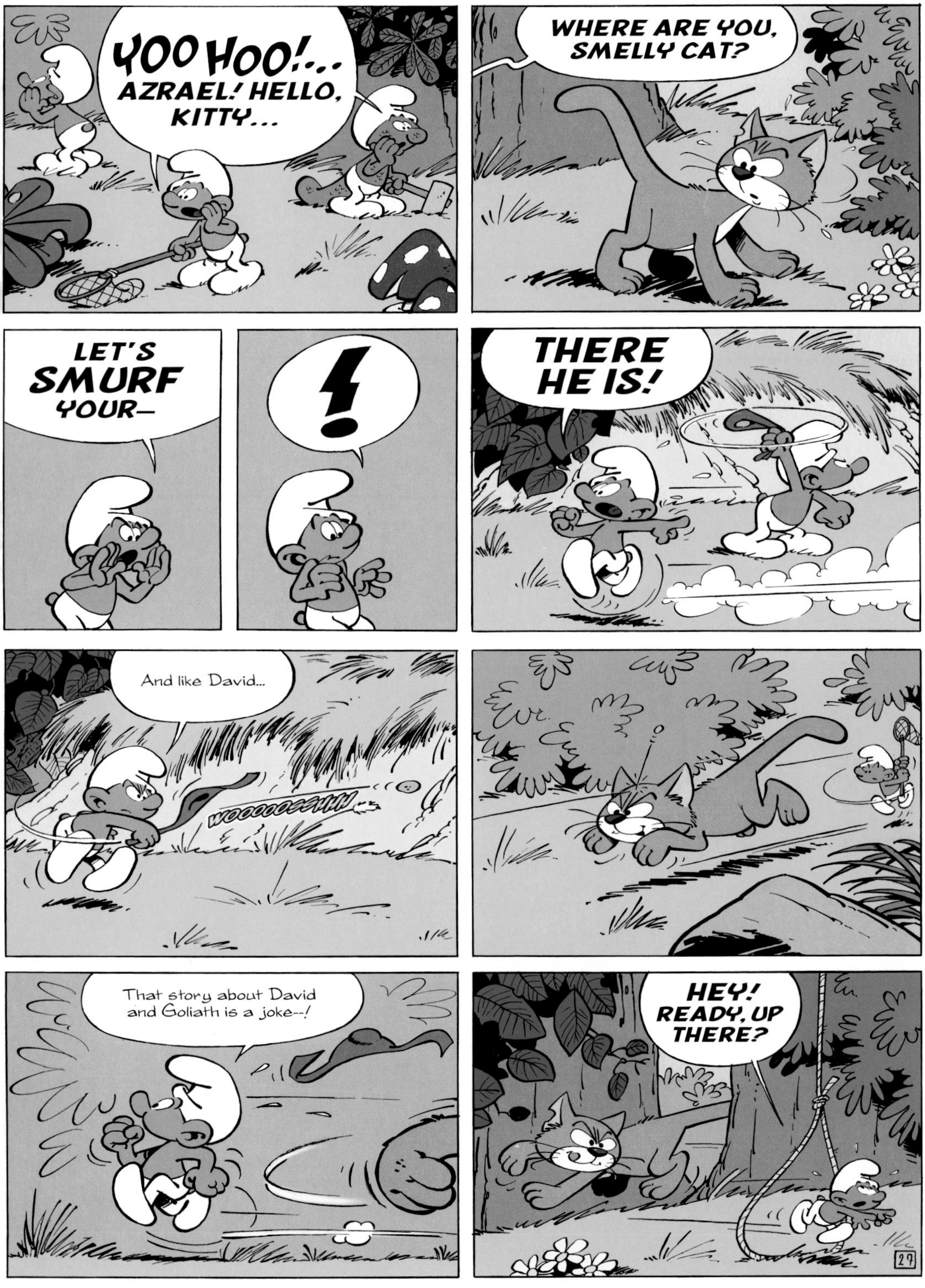
YOO HOO!... AZRAEL! HELLO, KITTY...
WHERE ARE YOU, SMELLY CAT?
LET'S SMURF YOUR—
!
THERE HE IS!
And like David...
WOOOOOSSHHH
That story about David and Goliath is a joke--!
HEY! READY, UP THERE?
27

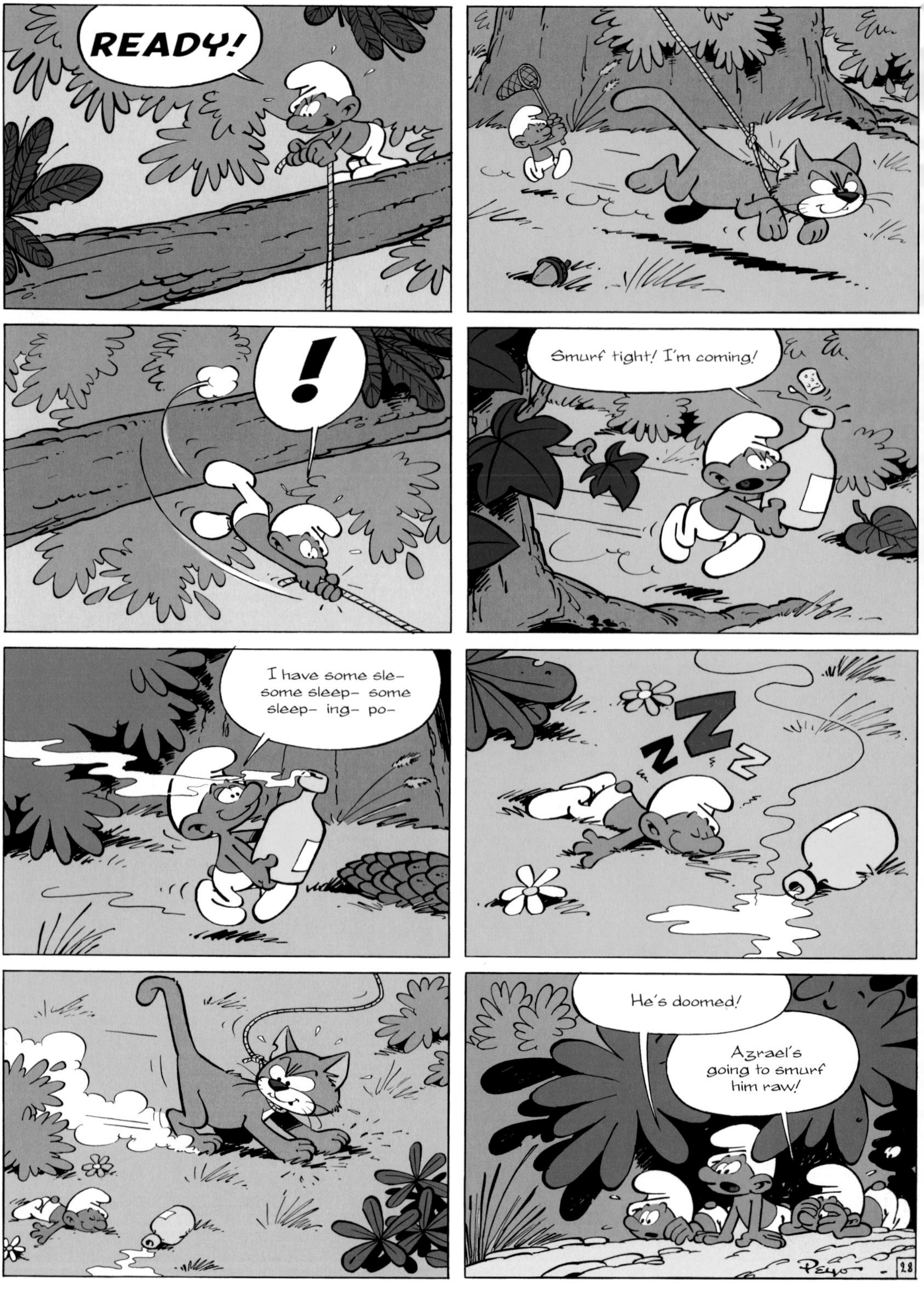
READY!
!
Smurf tight! I'm coming!
I have some sle- some sleep- some sleep- ing- po-
Z Z Z
He's doomed!
Azrael's going to smurf him raw!
PEYO
28

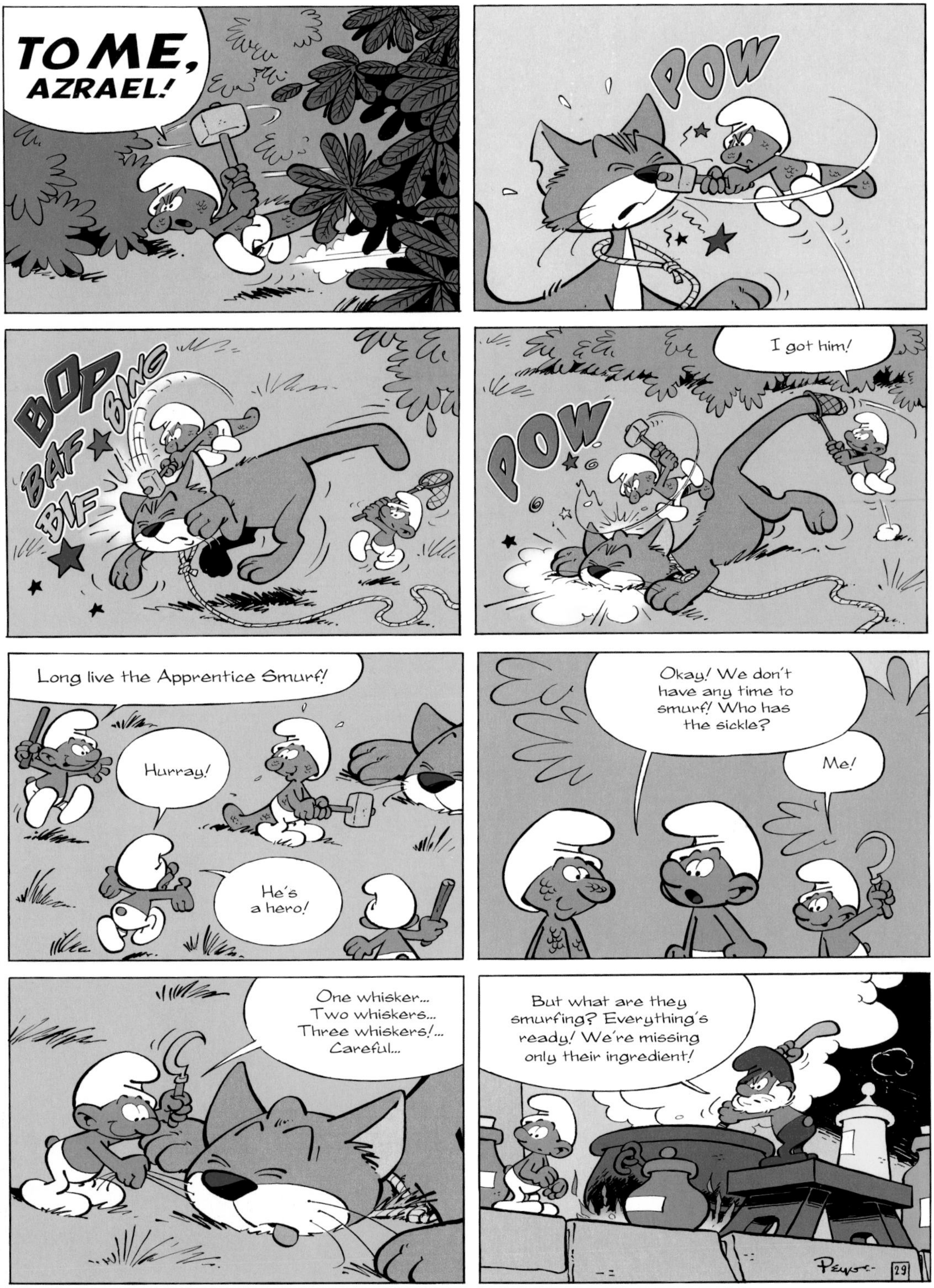
TO ME, AZRAEL!
POW
BOP
BAF
BING
BIF
POW
I got him!
Long live the Apprentice Smurf!
Hurray!
He's a hero!
Okay! We don't have any time to smurf! Who has the sickle?
Me!
One whisker... Two whiskers... Three whiskers!... Careful...
But what are they smurfing? Everything's ready! We're missing only their ingredient!
29

Here you go, Papa Smurf, we got them!

Good job! Give it to me... quick!

Hurry up! Gargamel smurfed slightly!

There! It's ready! Here, drink!

⸨Gluggluggluggclugg⸩

YIPPEE! HE'S SMURFED!

There's no reason to smurf here any longer! Let's quickly smurf back to the village!

I... I have... ⸨Humpf!⸩... I have to crack... ⸨Hmf!⸩... this glue...

CRRR

GRRR GRRR

THAT'S IT!

GR AAAK

REVENGE!

Where are they? It's not possible-- they've already disappeared!

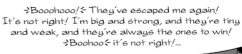

♪Booohooo!← They've escaped me again! It's not right! I'm big and strong, and they're tiny and weak, and they're always the ones to win! ♪Boohoo← it's not right!...

A few days have passed... Everything's back to normal.

Hey, how about I smurf a little chat with the Apprentice Smurf!?

!

PEYO

Smurf everything well with the help of a spatula! Next...

31

Oh, no! I have to warn Papa Smurf!

Yes, Papa Smurf, I saw him! Once again, he's busy smurfing a magic potion!

Ah! But this isn't going to smurf like last time! Where is he?

His home!

Come in!

KNOCK KNOCK KNOCK

Well? So you didn't learn your lesson? Are you starting to smurf magic again?

Why, no, Papa Smurf, it's not a magic recipe! It's the recipe for a smurf baba!

Peyo 32

THE END

SMURF TRAPS

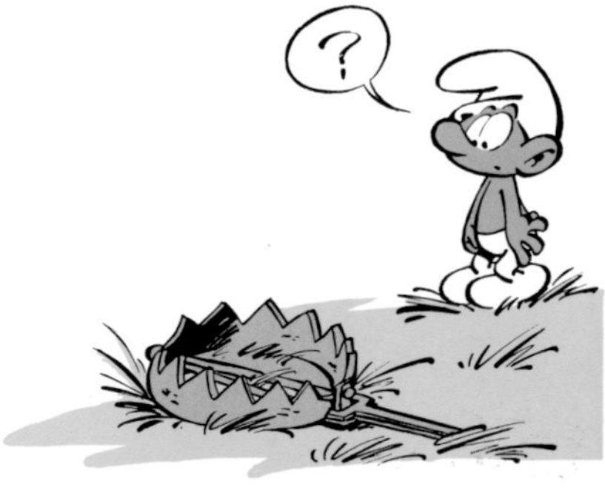
?

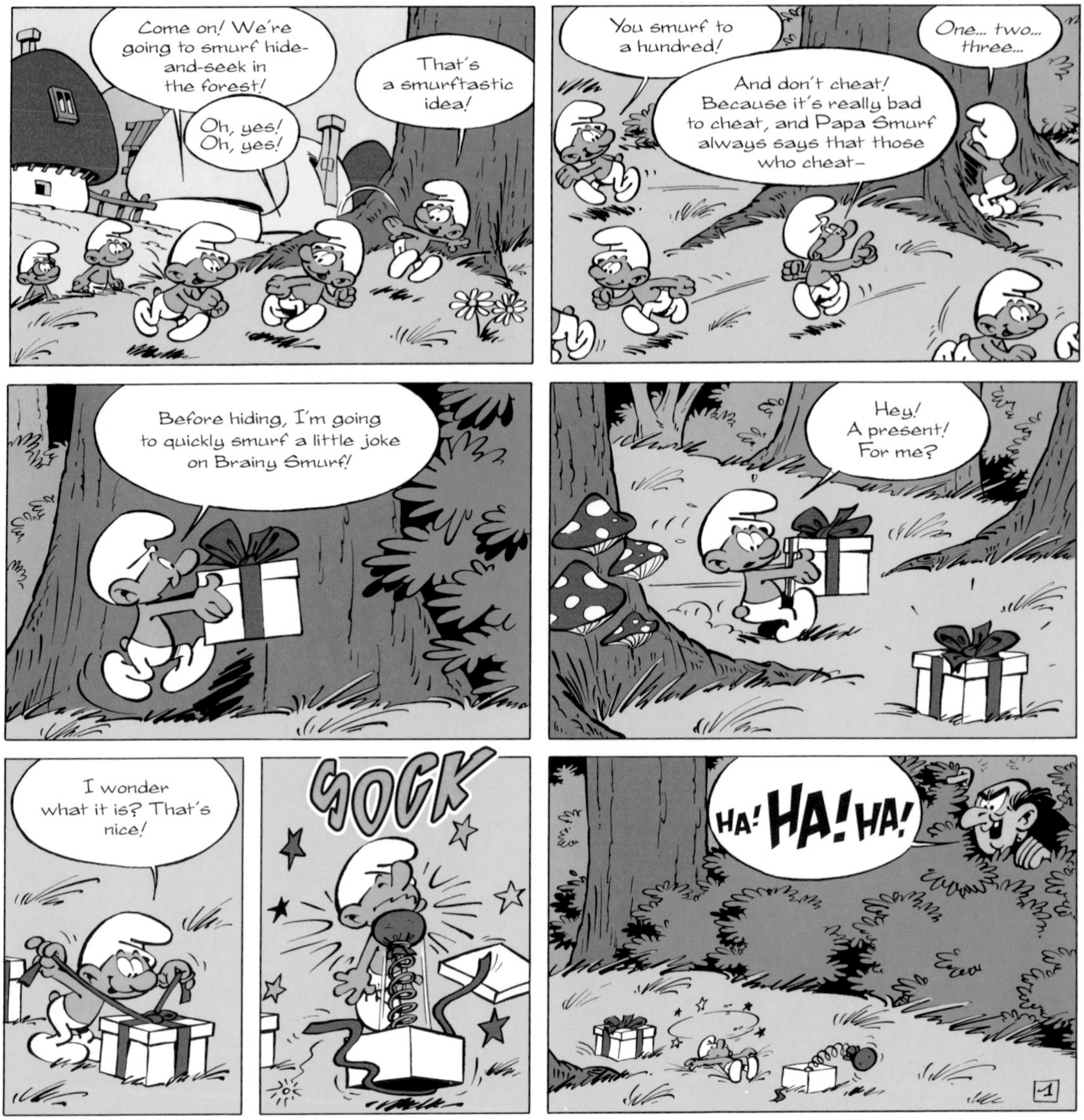
Come on! We're going to smurf hide-and-seek in the forest!
Oh, yes! Oh, yes!
That's a smurftastic idea!
You smurf to a hundred!
And don't cheat! Because it's really bad to cheat, and Papa Smurf always says that those who cheat–
One... two... three...
Before hiding, I'm going to quickly smurf a little joke on Brainy Smurf!
Hey! A present! For me?
I wonder what it is? That's nice!
SOCK
HA! HA! HA!

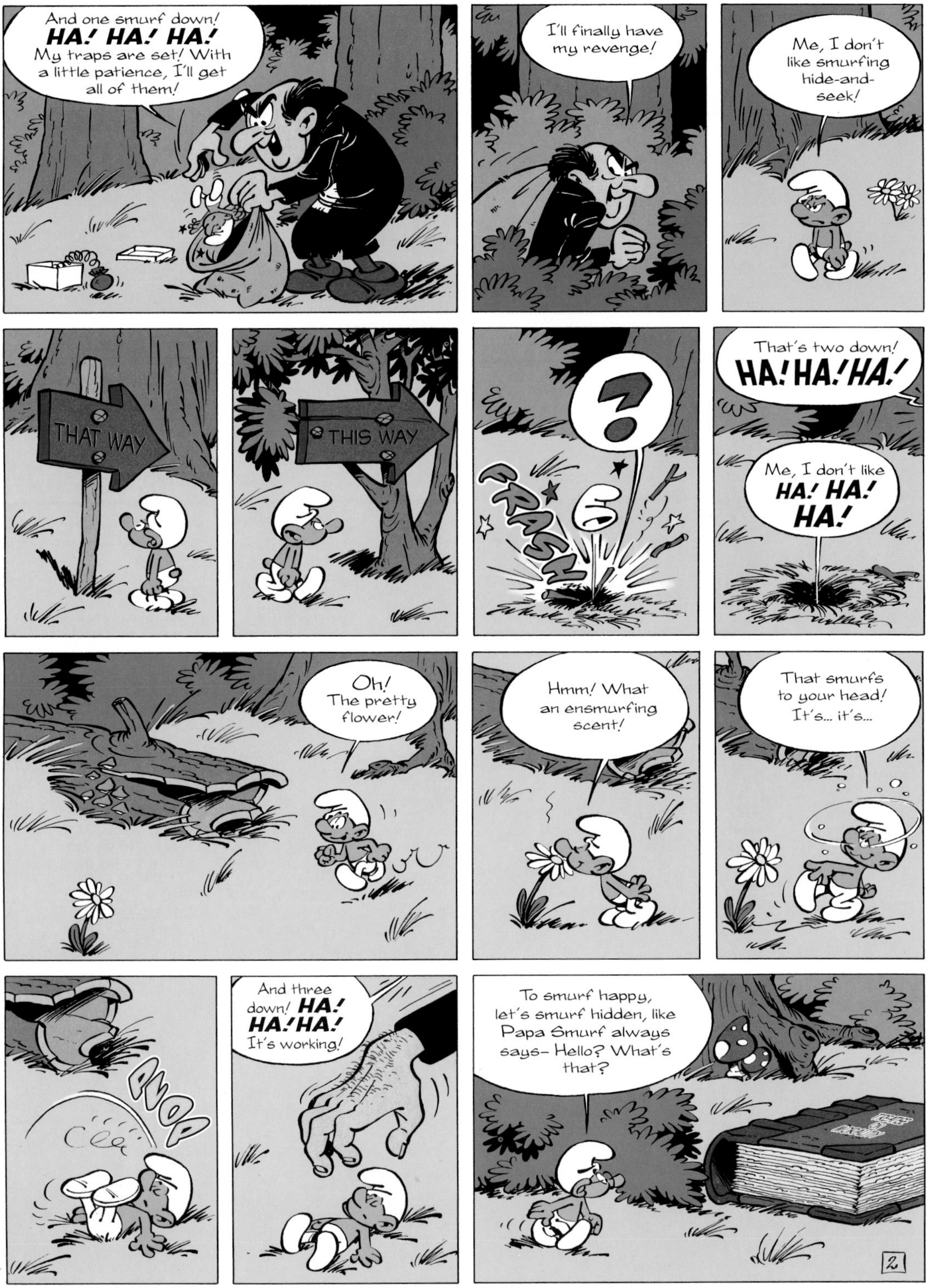
And one smurf down! HA! HA! HA! My traps are set! With a little patience, I'll get all of them!
I'll finally have my revenge!
Me, I don't like smurfing hide-and-seek!
THAT WAY
THIS WAY
?
CRASH
That's two down! HA! HA! HA!
Me, I don't like HA! HA! HA!
Oh! The pretty flower!
Hmm! What an ensmurfing scent!
That smurfs to your head! It's... it's...
And three down! HA! HA! HA! It's working!
To smurf happy, let's smurf hidden, like Papa Smurf always says– Hello? What's that?
2

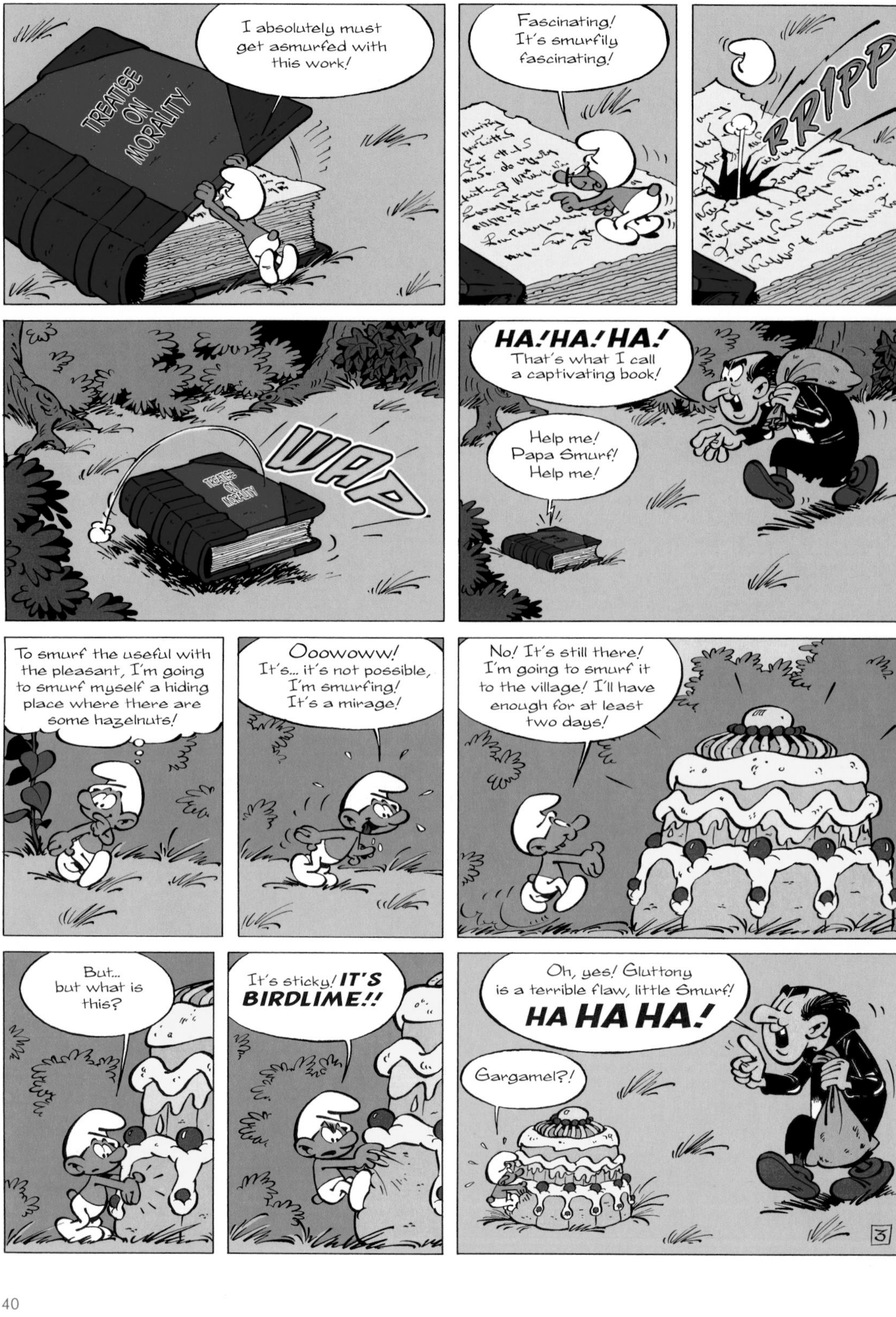
I absolutely must get asmurfed with this work!
TREATISE ON MORALITY
Fascinating! It's smurfily fascinating!
RRIPP
WAP
HA! HA! HA! That's what I call a captivating book!
Help me! Papa Smurf! Help me!
To smurf the useful with the pleasant, I'm going to smurf myself a hiding place where there are some hazelnuts!
Ooowoww! It's... it's not possible, I'm smurfing! It's a mirage!
No! It's still there! I'm going to smurf it to the village! I'll have enough for at least two days!
But... but what is this?
It's sticky! IT'S BIRDLIME!!
Oh, yes! Gluttony is a terrible flaw, little Smurf! HA HA HA!
Gargamel?!
3

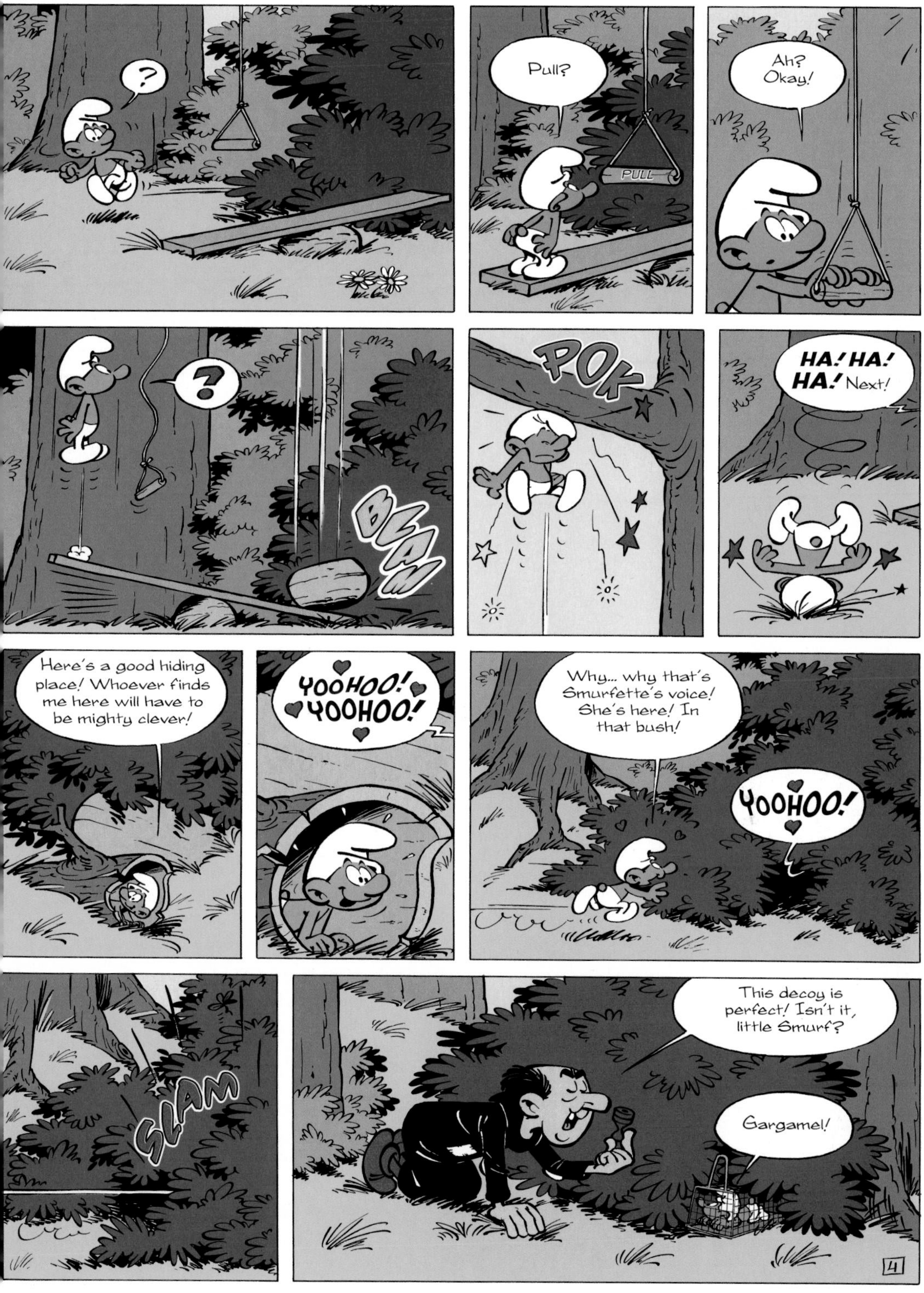
?
Pull?
PULL
Ah? Okay!
?
BLAM
POK
HA! HA! HA! Next!
Here's a good hiding place! Whoever finds me here will have to be mighty clever!
YOOHOO! YOOHOO!
Why... why that's Smurfette's voice! She's here! In that bush!
YOOHOO!
SLAM
This decoy is perfect! Isn't it, little Smurf?
Gargamel!
4

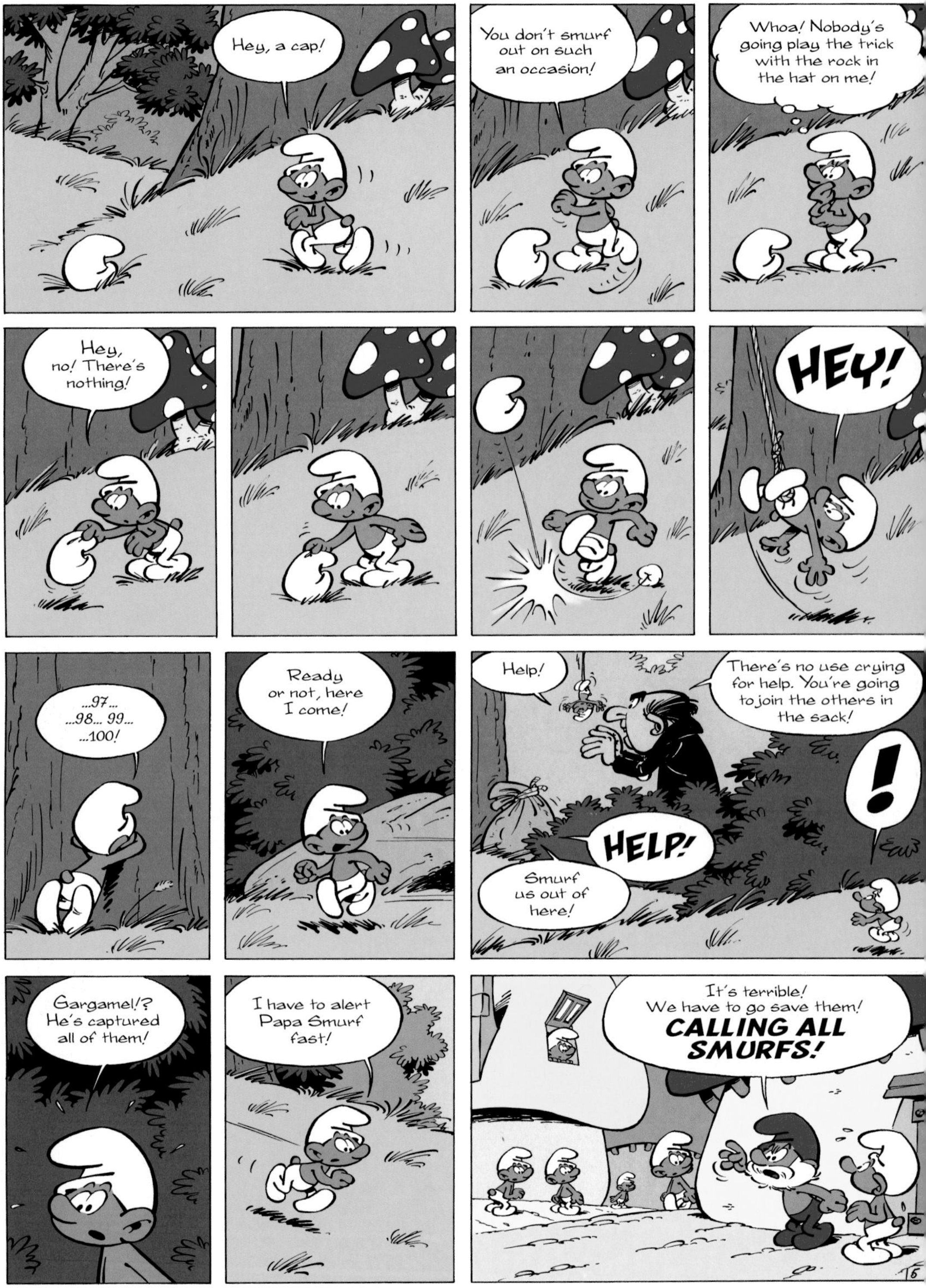

Hey, a cap!
You don't smurf out on such an occasion!
Whoa! Nobody's going play the trick with the rock in the hat on me!
Hey, no! There's nothing!
HEY!
...97... ...98... 99... ...100!
Ready or not, here I come!
Help!
There's no use crying for help. You're going to join the others in the sack!
!
HELP!
Smurf us out of here!
Gargamel!? He's captured all of them!
I have to alert Papa Smurf fast!
It's terrible! We have to go save them! CALLING ALL SMURFS!

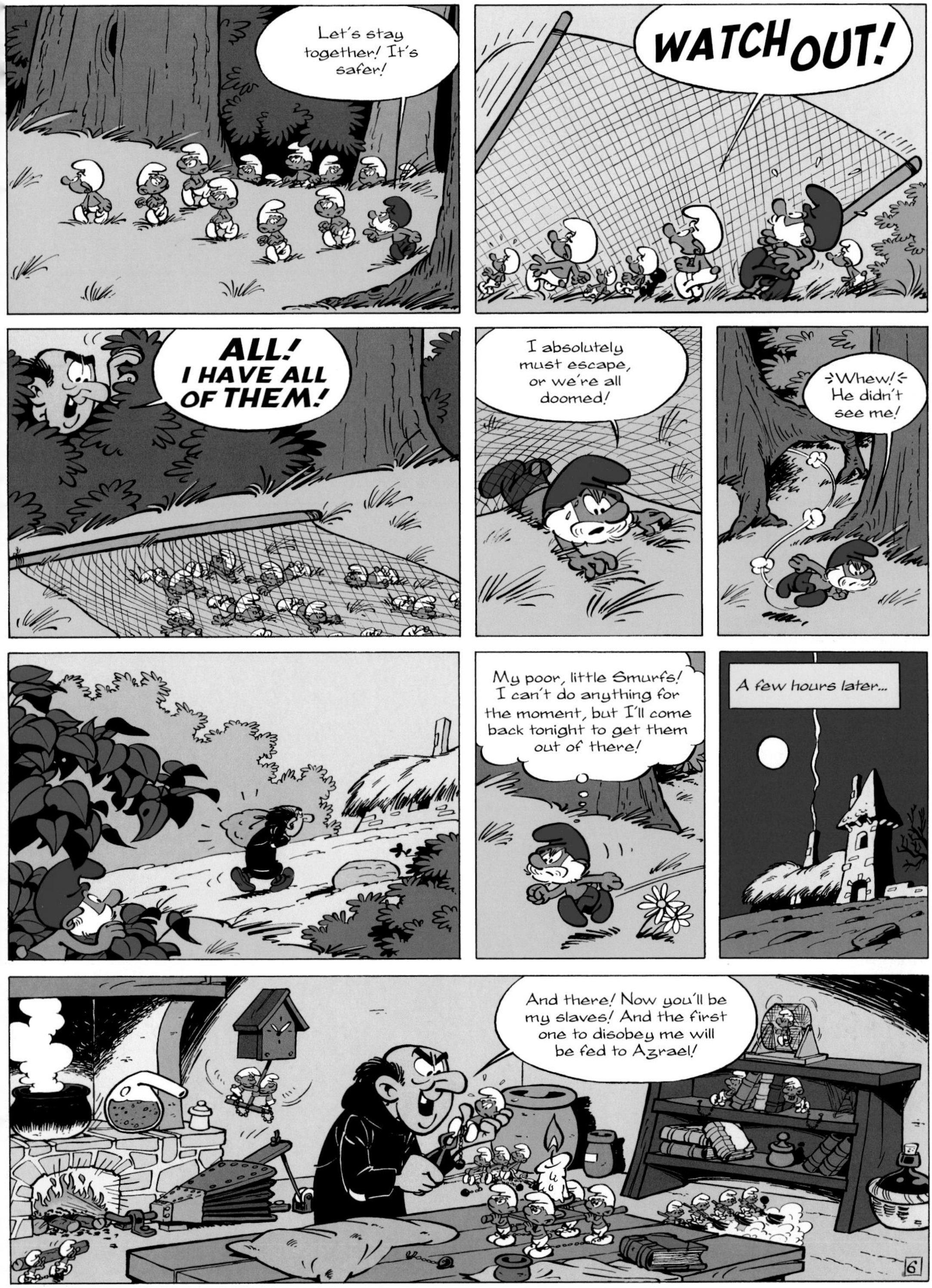
Let's stay together! It's safer!
WATCH OUT!
ALL! I HAVE ALL OF THEM!
I absolutely must escape, or we're all doomed!
Whew! He didn't see me!
My poor, little Smurfs! I can't do anything for the moment, but I'll come back tonight to get them out of there!
A few hours later...
And there! Now you'll be my slaves! And the first one to disobey me will be fed to Azrael!
6

Hmm? I've got one chain left, and the sack's empty! How's that possible?

PAPA SMURF!

I'm missing Papa Smurf!

Okay! He'll get his comeuppance! I'll take care of him tomorrow!... For now I'm going to bed!

AZRAEL!

HEY!

Since I can't trust you, you'll spend the night in the basement! Go on!

Ah! The light's out! Gargamel must have gone to bed! I can go in!

I must not fail, the lives of my little Smurfs depend on me!

Papa Smurf! Quick, come and rescue us!

Hush!

First I have to deal with Gargamel! But where's Azrael?

In the basement!

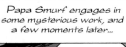

Papa Smurf engages in some mysterious work, and a few moments later...

Yoohoo! Gargamel!

Huh?... What?... What's going on?

But... what's that?

44

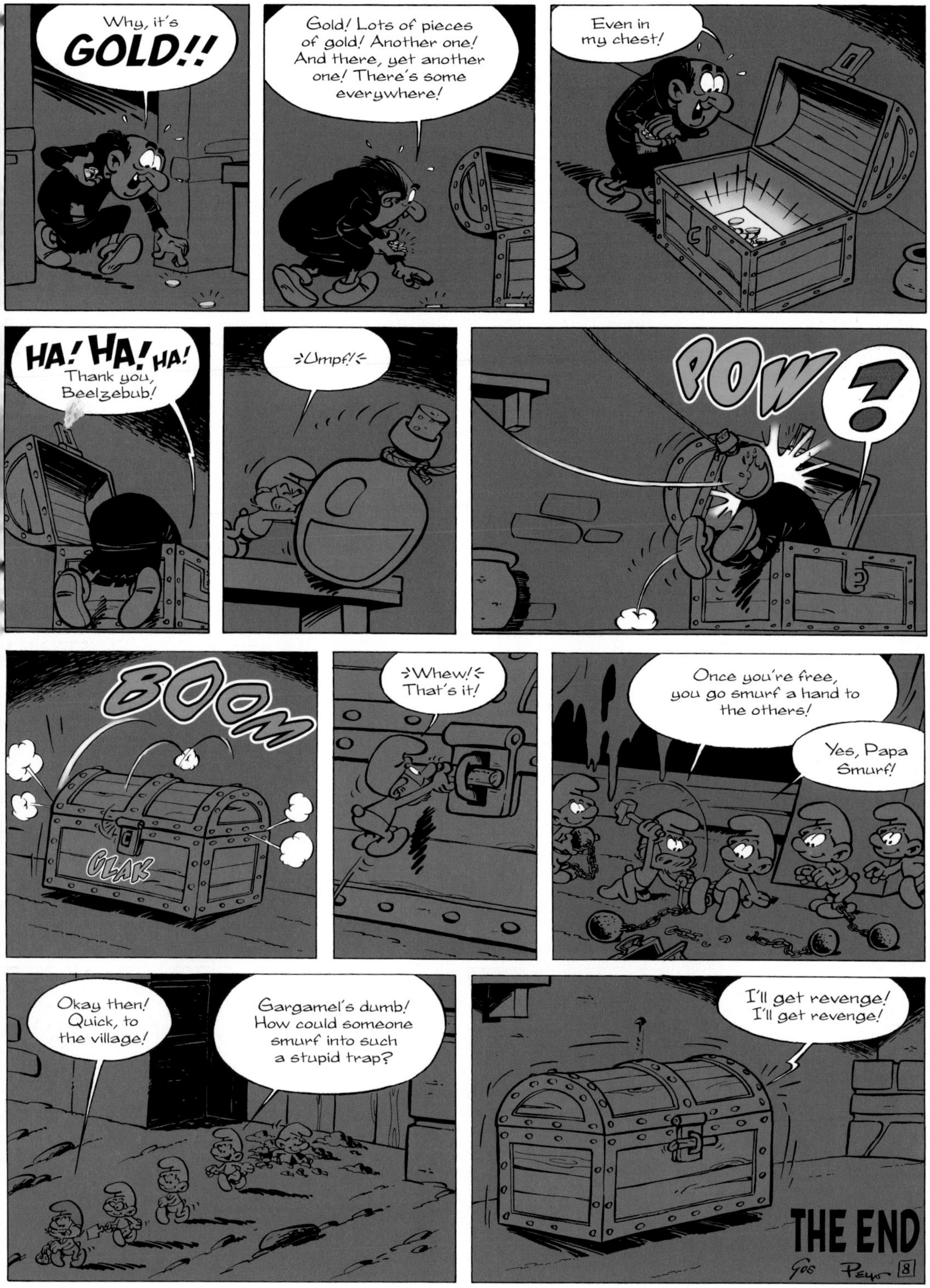

Why, it's GOLD!!
Gold! Lots of pieces of gold! Another one! And there, yet another one! There's some everywhere!
Even in my chest!
HA! HA! HA! Thank you, Beelzebub!
Umpf!
POW
?
BOOM
CLAK
Whew! That's it!
Once you're free, you go smurf a hand to the others!
Yes, Papa Smurf!
Okay then! Quick, to the village!
Gargamel's dumb! How could someone smurf into such a stupid trap?
I'll get revenge! I'll get revenge!
THE END
8

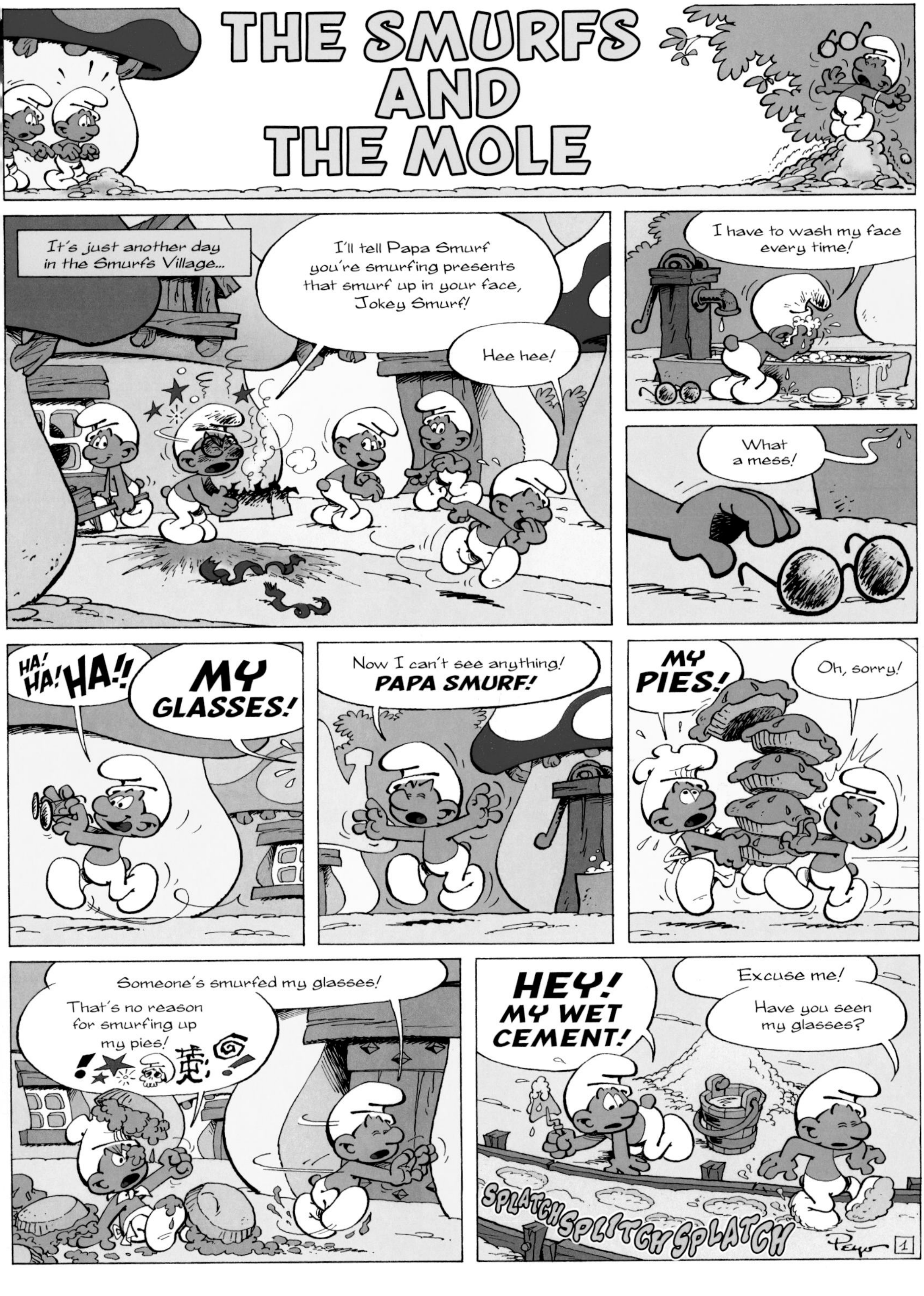
THE SMURFS AND THE MOLE
It's just another day in the Smurfs Village...
I'll tell Papa Smurf you're smurfing presents that smurf up in your face, Jokey Smurf!
Hee hee!
I have to wash my face every time!
What a mess!
HA! HA! HA!!
MY GLASSES!
Now I can't see anything! PAPA SMURF!
MY PIES!
Oh, sorry!
Someone's smurfed my glasses!
That's no reason for smurfing up my pies!
HEY! MY WET CEMENT!
Excuse me!
Have you seen my glasses?
SPLATCH SPLITCH SPLATCH
Peyo
1

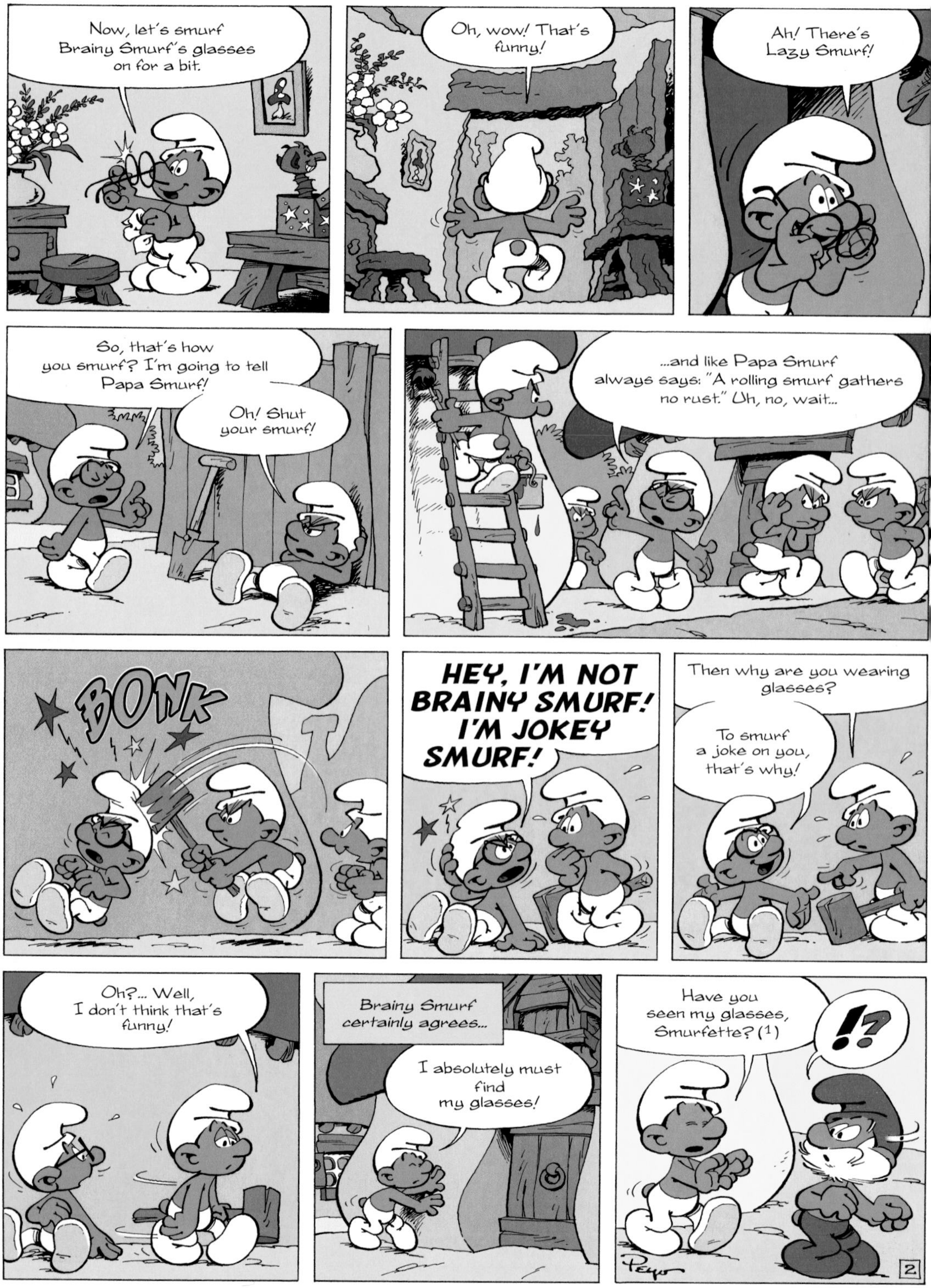
Now, let's smurf Brainy Smurf's glasses on for a bit.
Oh, wow! That's funny!
Ah! There's Lazy Smurf!
So, that's how you smurf? I'm going to tell Papa Smurf!
Oh! Shut your smurf!
...and like Papa Smurf always says: "A rolling smurf gathers no rust." Uh, no, wait...
BONK
HEY, I'M NOT BRAINY SMURF! I'M JOKEY SMURF!
Then why are you wearing glasses?
To smurf a joke on you, that's why!
Oh?... Well, I don't think that's funny!
Brainy Smurf certainly agrees...
I absolutely must find my glasses!
Have you seen my glasses, Smurfette? (1)
!?
Peyo
2

(1) The Smurfette hasn't been seen since THE SMURFS #4 "The Smurfette"!

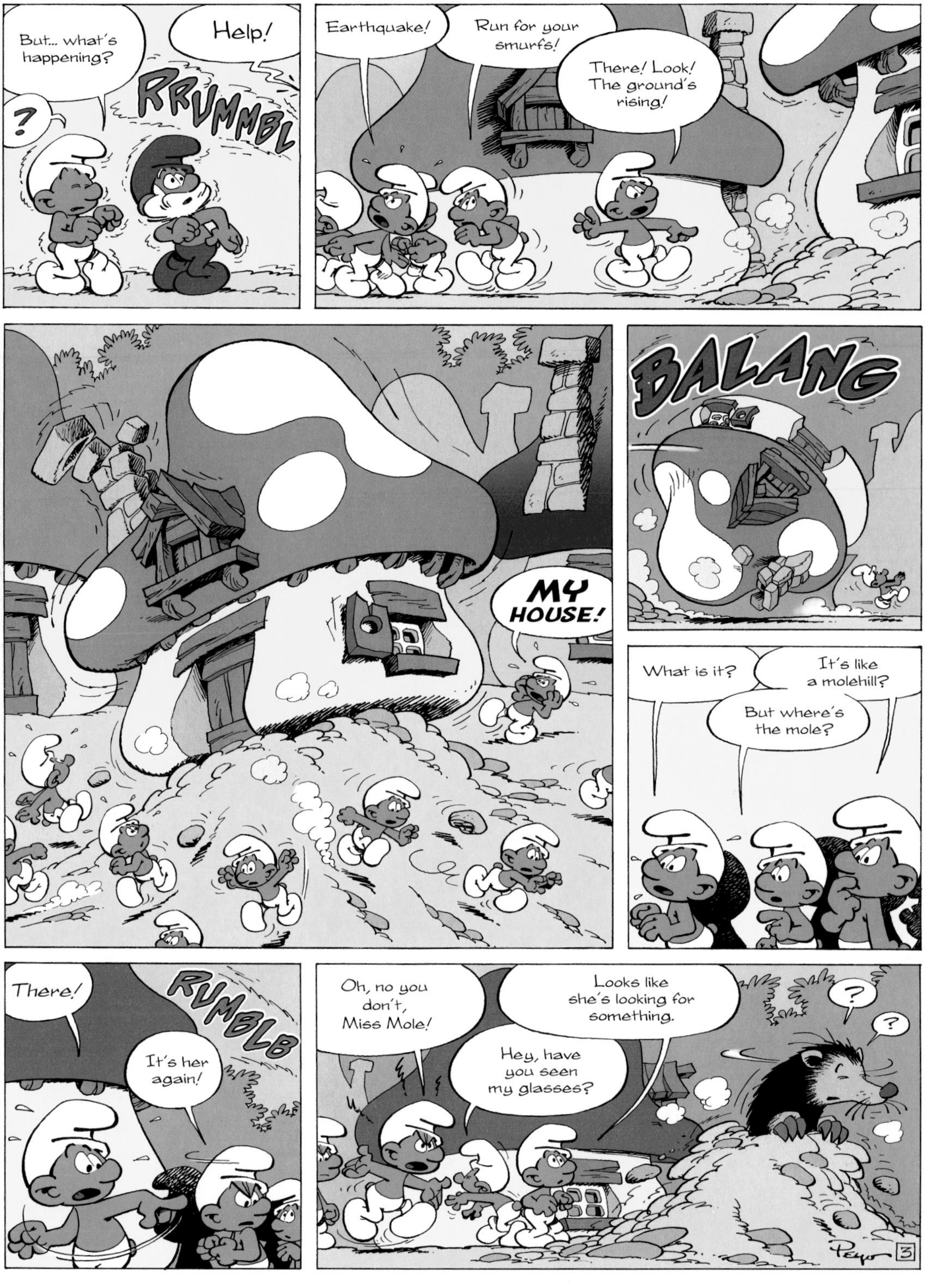
But... what's happening?
Help!
RRUMMBL
?
Earthquake!
Run for your smurfs!
There! Look! The ground's rising!
MY HOUSE!
BALANG
What is it?
It's like a molehill?
But where's the mole?
There!
RUMBLB
It's her again!
Oh, no you don't, Miss Mole!
Looks like she's looking for something.
Hey, have you seen my glasses?
?
?
Peyo
3

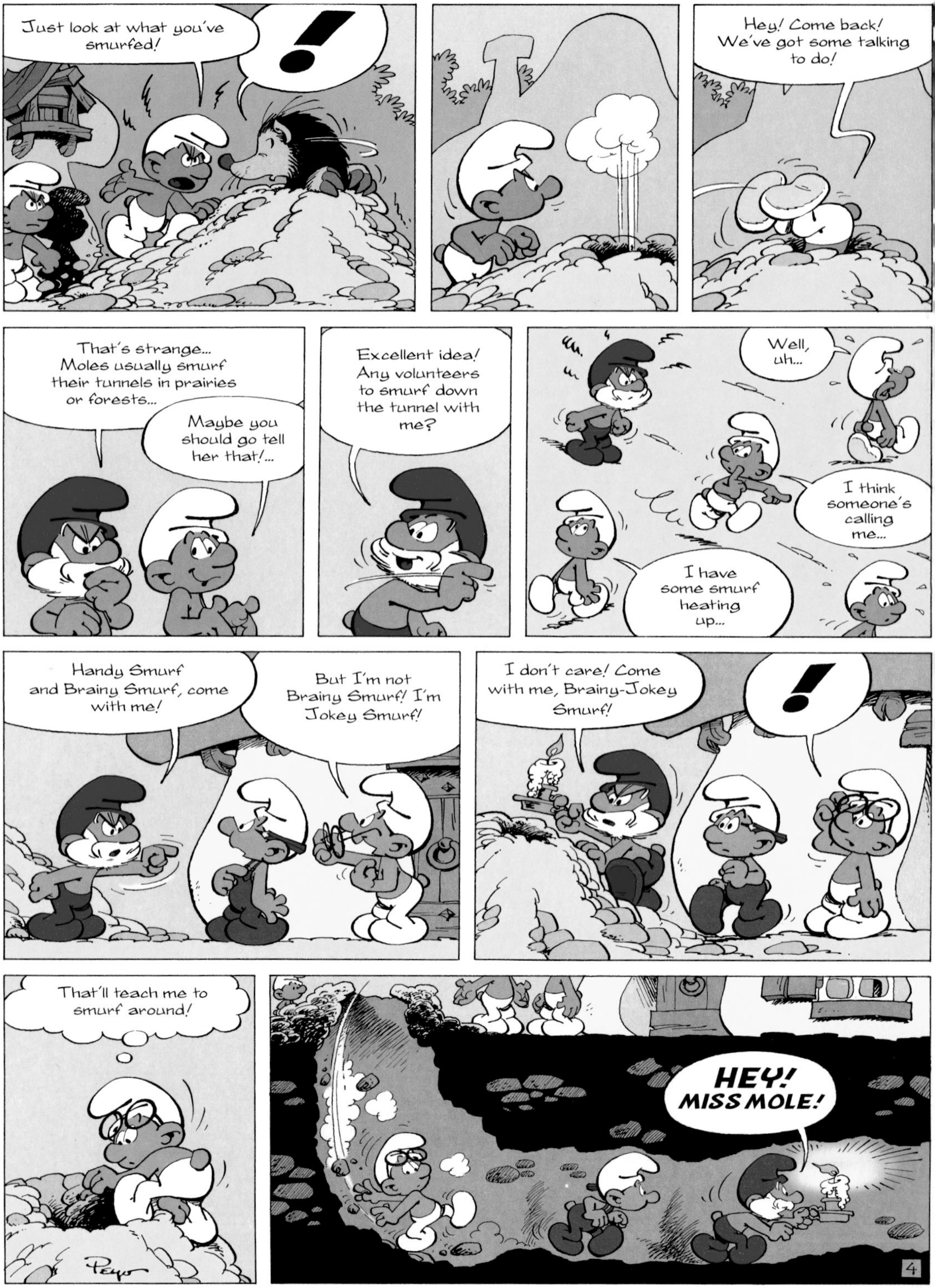
Just look at what you've smurfed!
!
Hey! Come back! We've got some talking to do!
That's strange... Moles usually smurf their tunnels in prairies or forests...
Maybe you should go tell her that!...
Excellent idea! Any volunteers to smurf down the tunnel with me?
Well, uh...
I think someone's calling me...
I have some smurf heating up...
Handy Smurf and Brainy Smurf, come with me!
But I'm not Brainy Smurf! I'm Jokey Smurf!
I don't care! Come with me, Brainy-Jokey Smurf!
!
That'll teach me to smurf around!
Peyo
HEY! MISS MOLE!
4

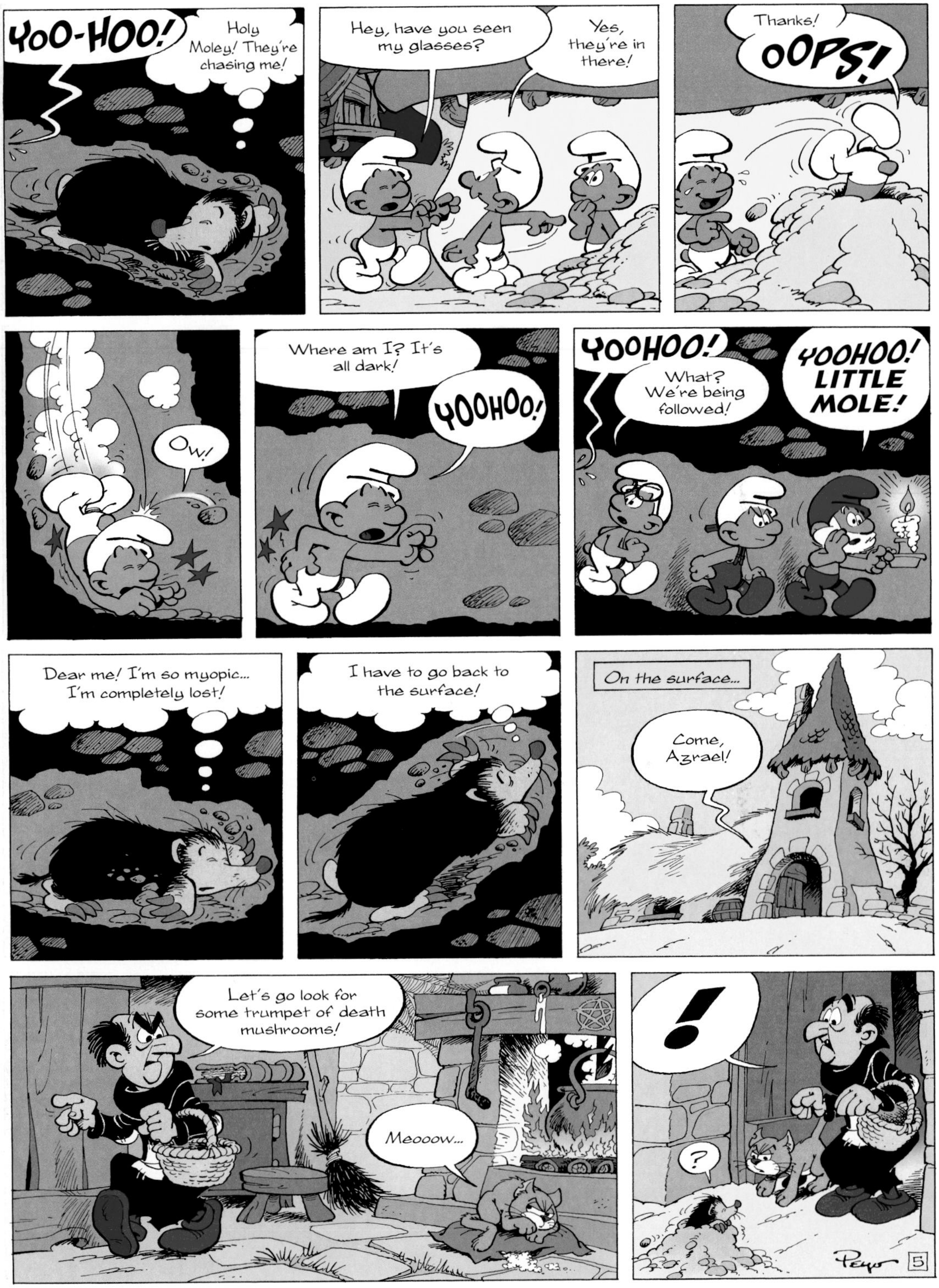
YOO-HOO!
Holy Moley! They're chasing me!
Hey, have you seen my glasses?
Yes, they're in there!
Thanks!
OOPS!
Ow!
Where am I? It's all dark!
YOOHOO!
YOOHOO!
What? We're being followed!
YOOHOO! LITTLE MOLE!
Dear me! I'm so myopic... I'm completely lost!
I have to go back to the surface!
On the surface...
Come, Azrael!
Let's go look for some trumpet of death mushrooms!
Meooow...
!
?
Peyo
5

A MOLE!

He's a crazy mean one!

I HAVE A FEAR OF MOLES!

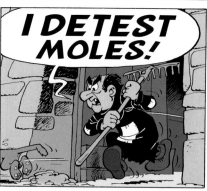

I DETEST MOLES!

I HATE MOLES!

WAM   WAM   WAM

OOPS! SORRY!

Ah! There you are! But can't you see where you're going?

Who is this fellow?

Excuse me, but without my glasses, I can't see anything here! I'm as nearsighted as a mole!

Like a... Good smurf! That's why this mole is digging tunnels all over the place! She's myopic! She needs glasses!

Here... take mine!

There's only one way to get that mole out of its hole! And that's my way!

6

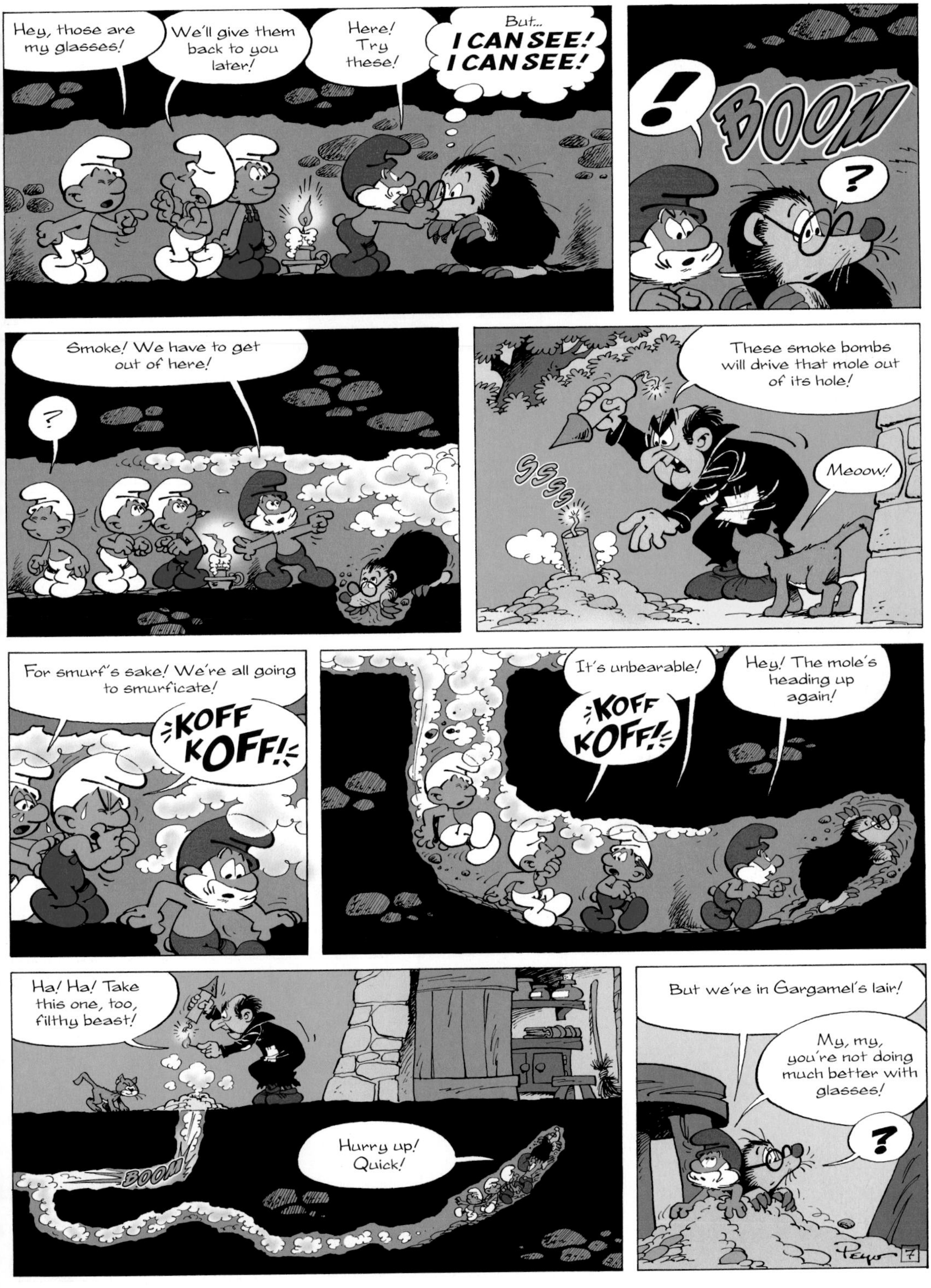

Hey, those are my glasses!
We'll give them back to you later!
Here! Try these!
But... I CAN SEE! I CAN SEE!
!
BOOM
?
Smoke! We have to get out of here!
?
These smoke bombs will drive that mole out of its hole!
SSSS
Meoow!
For smurf's sake! We're all going to smurficate!
KOFF KOFF!
It's unbearable!
KOFF KOFF!
Hey! The mole's heading up again!
Ha! Ha! Take this one, too, filthy beast!
BOOM
Hurry up! Quick!
But we're in Gargamel's lair!
My, my, you're not doing much better with glasses!
?
Peyo
7

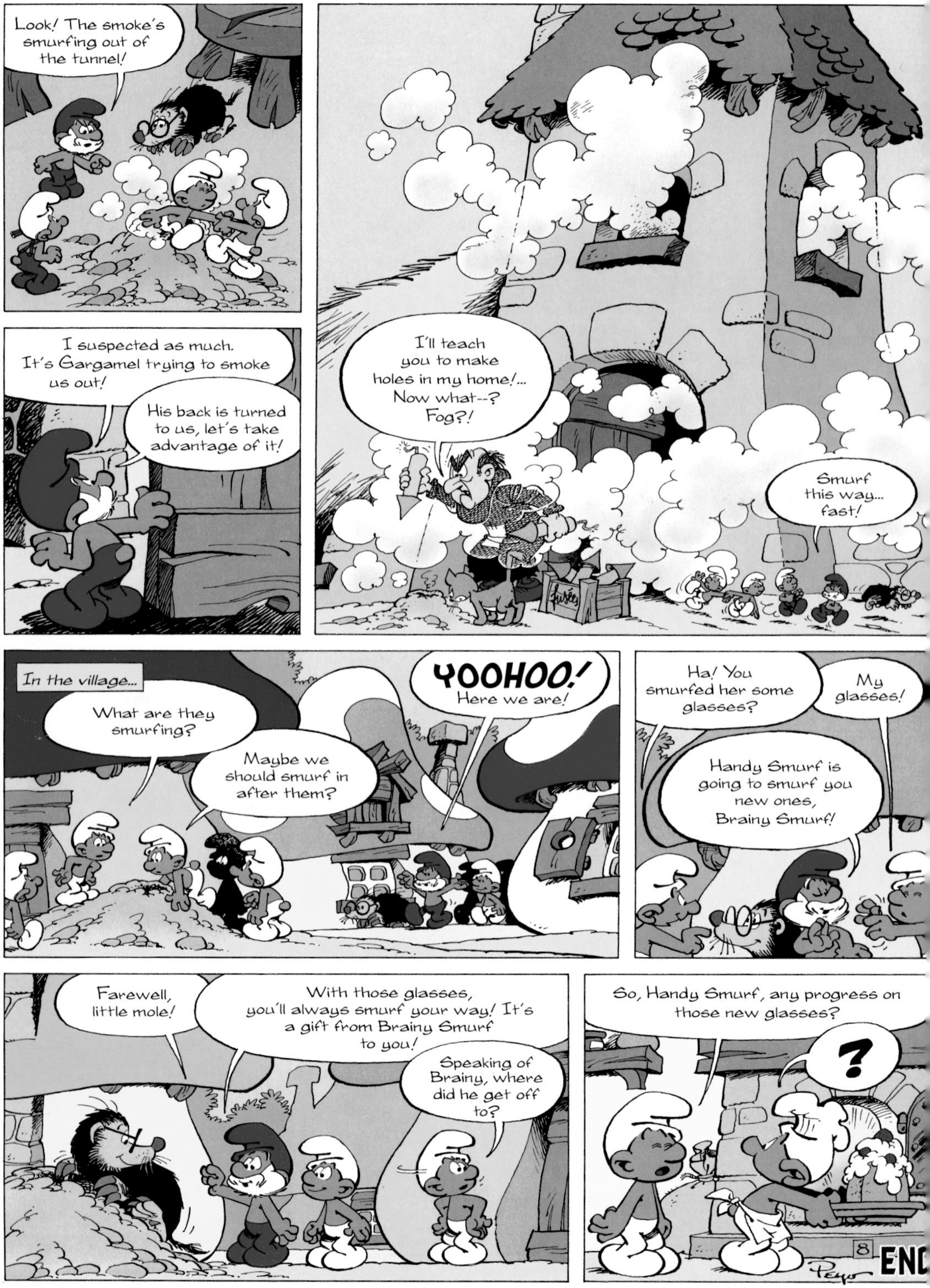
Look! The smoke's smurfing out of the tunnel!
I'll teach you to make holes in my home!... Now what--? Fog?!
I suspected as much. It's Gargamel trying to smoke us out!
His back is turned to us, let's take advantage of it!
Smurf this way... fast!
In the village...
What are they smurfing?
Maybe we should smurf in after them?
YOOHOO! Here we are!
Ha! You smurfed her some glasses?
My glasses!
Handy Smurf is going to smurf you new ones, Brainy Smurf!
Farewell, little mole!
With those glasses, you'll always smurf your way! It's a gift from Brainy Smurf to you!
Speaking of Brainy, where did he get off to?
So, Handy Smurf, any progress on those new glasses?
?
8
END

WATCH OUT FOR PAPERCUTZ™

Welcome to the enchanting and educational eighth SMURFS graphic novel from Papercutz, the mild-mannered publishers of great graphic novels for all ages. I'm Jim Salicrup, the apprehensive Smurf-in-Chief, wading his way through Gargamel's Smurf traps to tell you all the latest news from Papercutz. Well, I would if I had more room! But we squeeze in so many Smurfs in every SMURFS graphic novel that all I can do is suggest that you visit www.papercutz.com and check out all the exciting titles we produce, such as CLASSICS ILLUSTRATED, celebrating its big 70th anniversary; DISNEY FAIRIES, featuring Tinker Bell; GARFIELD & Co, based on the hit Cartoon Network TV series; GERONIMO STILTON, who's saving the future, by protecting the past; NANCY DREW, America's favorite Girl Detective; and PAPERCUTZ SLICES, the world's greatest series of parody graphic novels! We're also unleashing a slew of new titles soon, so be sure to keep an eye on our website!

In the meantime, I wanted to tell you about some of the folks responsible for bringing you these amazing SMURFS graphic novels. Obviously, the most important person of all is Peyo! Without him the world would be Smurfless— what a terrible thought! You can learn all about the creator of THE SMURFS in Matt. Murray's "The World of Smurfs: A Celebration of Tiny Blue Proportions," the book no true Smurfs-fan should be without. But let me tell you about some of the other folks who help produce the Papercutz editions. You might say it takes a village, a Smurfs Village, to assemble each SMURFS graphic novel. One such person is the award-winning designer Adam Grano.

There's an interesting story about how Adam got the assignment of Smurfic Designer. When he heard that Papercutz publisher Terry Nantier had acquired the North American publishing rights to THE SMURFS, Adam knew he had to do something special to get Terry's attention to make his pitch. After all, Adam lives about

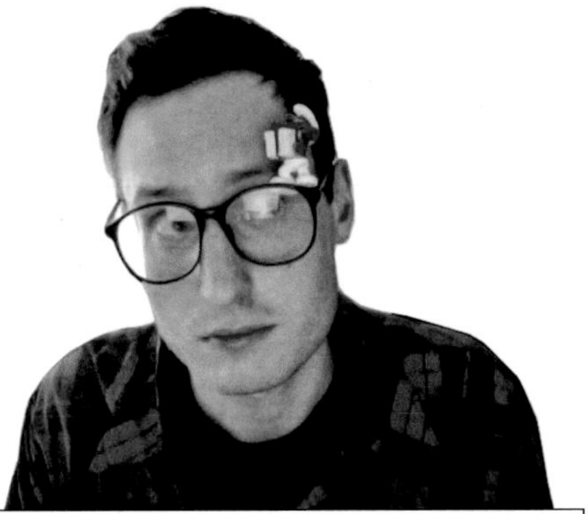

Smurfic Designer Adam Grano (and Jokey Smurf)

3,000 miles west from the palatial Papercutz offices. Adam posted a plea to Terry online at The Comics Journal website, a very popular site for serious comic art afficianados. Adam wrote, "...I'd like to make a public appeal to you to allow me to design [the] upcoming SMURFS books. If I'm too late with this appeal, then ... bummer, but I just heard about your project yesterday... If it helps, I would happily work for a pittance — this is the comics industry after all." Adam sure knows how to appeal to a publisher's heart... and purse! But what really sold us, aside from his incredible talent, was when Adam wrote...

"I just kinda love the Smurfs.

"That feels strange to say, but I really do have a soft spot for the little blue halflings. I grew up on them." Well, talk about an offer you can't refuse... ! Naturally, we contacted Adam and signed him up, and have been thrilled with the Smurftastic results!

We'll talk about more behind-the-scenes folks in the next "Watch Out for Papercutz" column in THE SMURFS #9 "Gargamel and the Smurfs," coming November 2011! See you then!

JIM

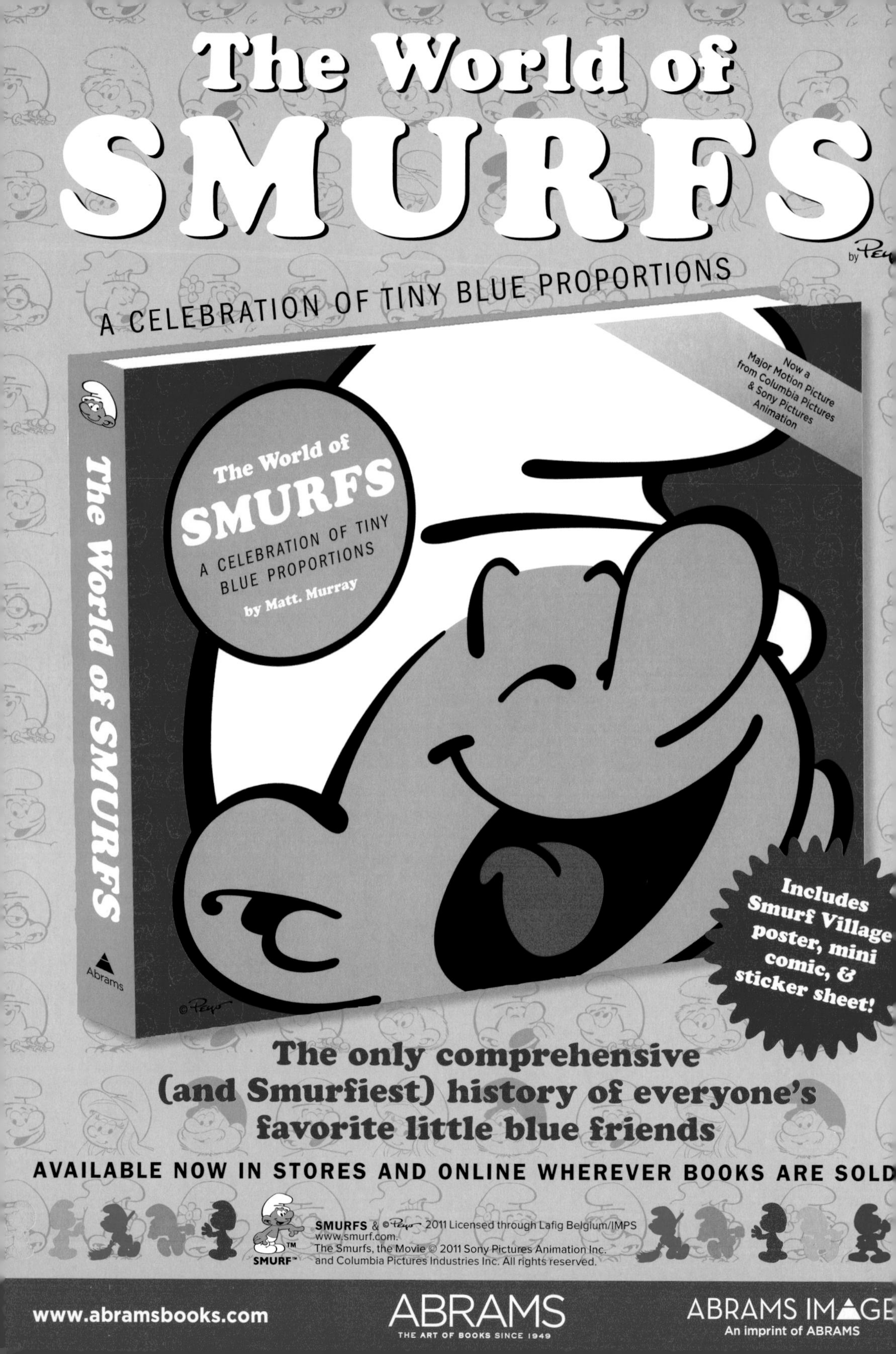
The World of
SMURFS
by Peyo
A CELEBRATION OF TINY BLUE PROPORTIONS
Now a Major Motion Picture from Columbia Pictures & Sony Pictures Animation
The World of SMURFS
The World of SMURFS
A CELEBRATION OF TINY BLUE PROPORTIONS
by Matt. Murray
Abrams
© Peyo
Includes Smurf Village poster, mini comic, & sticker sheet!
The only comprehensive (and Smurfiest) history of everyone's favorite little blue friends
AVAILABLE NOW IN STORES AND ONLINE WHEREVER BOOKS ARE SOLD
SMURF™
SMURFS & © Peyo 2011 Licensed through Lafig Belgium/IMPS
www.smurf.com.
The Smurfs, the Movie © 2011 Sony Pictures Animation Inc. and Columbia Pictures Industries Inc. All rights reserved.
www.abramsbooks.com
ABRAMS
THE ART OF BOOKS SINCE 1949
ABRAMS IMAGE
An imprint of ABRAMS

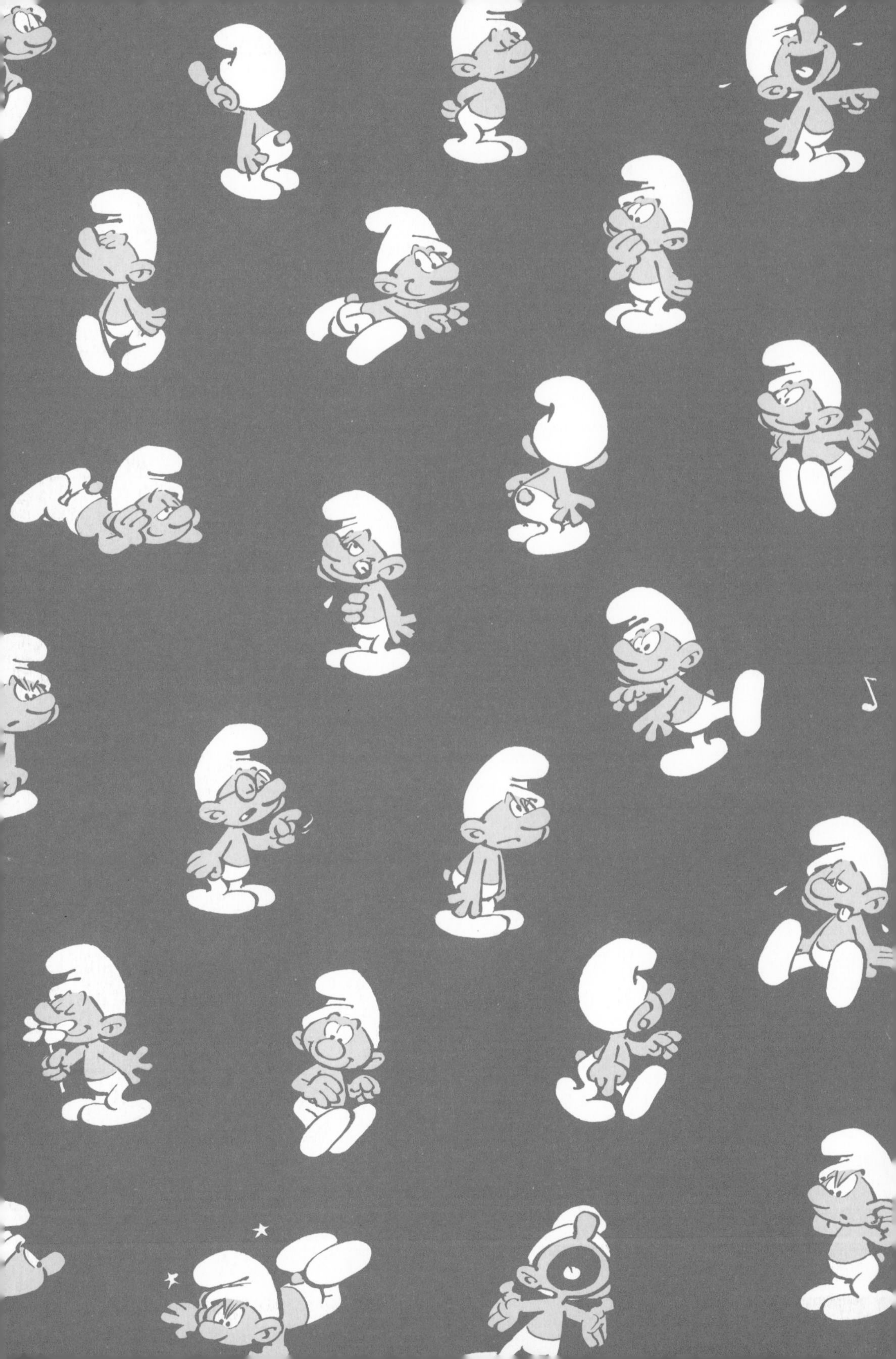